WATSON

WILKERSON DYNASTY Book 3

KATHI S. BARTON

This is a work of fiction. Names, characters, places, and incidents are products of the author's imagination or are used fictitiously and are not to be construed as real. Any resemblance to actual events, locations, organizations, or persons, living or dead, is entirely coincidental.

World Castle Publishing, LLC

Pensacola, Florida

Copyright © Kathi S. Barton 2021

Paperback ISBN: 9781953271990

eBook ISBN: 9781955086004

First Edition World Castle Publishing, LLC, April 12, 2021

http://www.worldcastlepublishing.com

Licensing Notes

Cover: Karen Fuller

Editor: Maxine Bringenberg

Prologue

Wats leaned back in his chair and closed his eyes. He loved being able to work for himself, but he'd been working much too hard. The family alone was keeping him hopping. Thinking of the conversation he'd had with his cousin Shawn today, he wondered what was going to happen to him when he figured out that life could throw you a curveball without any notice.

"I'm going to take some time off." Wats asked him what he was going to do that for. "I'm thinking if I don't get my home in order now, I'm going to be sitting here with an empty house when I'm sixty years old. Not that it's old, but the house is so empty, it's like living in a tomb."

"All right. Not that I think you'd need time off to buy some furniture, but I hope you get it done the way you want it." Shawn told him he was going to fill it with things he loved that he picked up at estate auctions. "Why? I mean, great, but why?"

"When was the last time you were at my parents' home?" Wats said he didn't remember. "Yeah, well, it's all steel and glass. I don't know if Dad even likes it. Anyway, I'm going to get things that speak to me. Dad is going to go on this trip with me. He's thinking he is going to love living in the condo. At least his brothers are close by, and he can walk to town if he wants. We're going to have some fun getting to know each other."

"Now, that I can get behind. What is your dad doing with his home?" Uncle Hank hadn't been in his house since Penny had been arrested. They all called her that now, and it was fun. "My dad is going to sell his as soon as he gets it emptied out. It seems none of them were very thrilled about returning to their homes."

"Dad is donating the house to the city. I haven't any idea what they're going to do with it—it's really run-down—but he gave them the property there too. That's about fifty acres. I'm thinking they're going to tear the house down then put in something equally ugly." No doubt. Wats told him about North's dad running for mayor. "He'd be really good at that. With as long as this family has lived here, he'd know just about anything and everything about the town."

Wats sat up when his phone rang. He thought he'd put it on the service, but he might not have gotten it right. There was a learning curve on just about everything he did lately. Saying his name, Wats waited while the person at the other end calmed down enough to speak.

"My grandfather is gone." Wats didn't know what she meant—gone as in missing or gone that he'd died. "He's not here. I came in this morning to stay with him while I finished up my classes, and we had a nice breakfast. Then when I went to the university to see about the classes I would need, I came home, and someone had been in here. There is blood all over the place too."

"Did you call the police?" There was a long pause, and Wats asked her again. "I don't even know who this is or what your grandfather's name is."

"My grandda is James Oliver. My name is Rayne Oliver. Why do you think he had your phone number in his phone marked as police?" Wats said that he didn't have any idea. "I'm going to call the police now. I'm so sorry to have bothered you."

"It's no trouble. I'm on my way there with my medical bag. When we find him, I'll be able to see how he's faring." He didn't want to say anything about him maybe being dead. Lots of blood could be scary enough. "I'm going to call my cousins in too. All of us can look for him."

Wats called the others and told them what was going on. He also mentioned how his number was listed as the emergency number. He called North last, as his number had been busy when he'd called him the first time.

"He's with me at my house." Wats turned his car around and headed toward North's home. "As for the blood, I don't know. There wasn't any there when the two of us left there a few hours ago."

"She said there was a great deal of it." Wats parked in the parking lot of the store he was nearby and tried to catch his breath. "What should I do? Go there and find out what is happening or just go back to my offices?"

"Why don't you go and see if you can talk to Rayne in person? Then perhaps bring her to my house. I don't think she should be driving if she's that upset." Wats told him he'd go out there now. "Be careful, Wats. Since we have no idea what the blood is from, someone might still be in the house."

"Well, thank you very much for that thought."

He made his way to the house carefully. There didn't seem to be any cars along the way that were parked without anyone in them. Nor did he see any indication of trouble. By the time he was pulling up in front of the house, there were two cruisers there, and a young woman on the front porch rocking in the rocker set out there.

"Your cousin called here. He told me that my grandda was with him." Wats told her he'd take her there if she wanted to go. "I do. I hope you don't mind, but I have to wait on the police. They're doing their thing in there now. I was terrified."

Wats checked her over. He told her he didn't want anything to be wrong with her and checked not just her blood pressure, which was just a little high, but her temperature too. When he was able to give her a clean bill of health, he sat down on the porch in front of her.

"I've known your grandda for a while. When I was in med school, he was one of the free patients that, as students, we were to work with. He's a very healthy man for his age." Rayne told him he didn't sit around on his duff like a lot of people his age. "I think I remember him being about eighty? I could be wrong."

"He'll be ninety-three on his next birthday. Which is coming up. He's all I care about in the world now. My parents are both gone. I don't have any sisters or brothers. No aunts that I want to be around either." She laughed. "The last time I was here, he and his sister, my aunt Carol, had this big to do about him living alone. Christ, he's a few years older than her and looks like he could be her kid. Not really, but Grandda is in really wonderful shape."

Wats told her about the house that was going to be built for him and how his cousin, North, was going to make sure he was going to be all right living out here alone. Rayne told him she had planned on living with him until she graduated next year, then she was hoping she could get him to move in with her.

"I've had a little house since my parents died. It's not much, but it's a damned sight better than this is. I guess North, as you called him, saw what he was living in here." Wats told her how he'd only just bought the house a few weeks ago. "The banker that was holding the place didn't want to do anything for him. Told my grandda he'd be better off in a nursing home if he didn't like this place. Grandda lost Grannie here. He doesn't want to leave without going to her, he told me."

By the time the police were finished up with the house, they'd discovered that a raccoon had made its way into the house when it had been attacked by something larger. The blood was all animal blood.

It was confirmed it was a raccoon when they found his body in the bedroom that Grandda used.

"I think he's been feeding the poor thing. Grandda is allergic to cats and doesn't care for dogs. They're too big for him to handle, he told me. But this little raccoon made his way into his heart, and he's been taking care of him. I think it was making the loneliness more tolerable." Wats thought that was the nicest thing he'd heard in a while. "I don't know if we'll be able to stay here now. At least not tonight."

"I have a condo you can stay in. I mean by yourself. With your grandda. I'll be someplace else." Wats let out a long breath. "I have a furnished condo the two of you can stay in. I'll bunk with my dad. He's close to where you two can stay."

"I don't want to put you out." Wats assured her she wouldn't be. He was enjoying spending time with his dad. "If you're sure?"

"I am sure. You gather up some things for him to wear, and tomorrow we'll come back here to see what we can salvage out of the bedroom. After that, North is going to take care of getting something more livable in here for the two of you." Wats hoped his dad didn't mind him staying with him a few days. "You get some things, like I said, and I'll make a couple of calls. That way, by the time you're finished here, I can have my arrangements made as well."

As he figured, Dad was happy to have him. North said he was his hero for doing this. All Wats had wanted to do was go to bed and not wake up anytime soon. It was stressful being the worrier of the family. Taking Rayne to his brother's house, then to the condo, was about all he could handle this evening. Going to his dad's condo, Wats was thrilled that he didn't seem to mind him rushing off to bed and let Wats go without bombarding him with questions.

As soon as his head hit the pillow, Wats knew he wasn't far from sleep. When a phone rang somewhere in the place, he had to catch himself from getting up and answering it. Being dead tired as he was, he didn't think he could make a sound decision on whether or not he liked chocolate ice cream or vanilla. Or even both, for that matter.

Thinking briefly of the list he'd brought from his office, Wats wondered if any of the others would help him out with it. He needed someone to work for him to answer phones. To clean up after him and his patients. Also, Wats needed to get laid.

Laughing a little, he rolled to his side and smiled. Tomorrow was going to be a brand new day, and he was going to try his best not to be running all over town again. Yes, he thought as slumber took him under, tomorrow was a brand new day.

Chapter 1

Wats didn't want to be there. He supposed no one wanted to be there that was related to his mother. But if he had to do this, he thought whoever had come up with this plan of doing it via a remote location was brilliant. Wats had been called in as a witness, and to him, not having to see his mother or any of his aunts was the best news he could have had today. Things so far, he thought, were going according to plan.

"What the hell is going on? Where is my son and husband?" Wats didn't bother answering his mother, as he was told he didn't have to. "Watson Wilkerson, you had better be thinking about how much punishment you're going to get when I get out of here. And once I do, you can also bet I'm not going to go easy on either of you. Why the hell aren't you in here where I can see you?"

"Because I have no desire to see you. Just shut up, and this will be over soon." He knew as soon as he told her to shut up that it would piss her off. Not that he cared. Not anymore. "Besides, I'm only here so I can testify, then I'm gone."

"You had better keep your mouth shut on things you think you know. Or I swear to you, Watson, I'll make you wish you'd never been born. Just as much as I wish that daily. Where is your father? Why isn't he working on getting me out of here?"

Done with her, he watched as the camera spanned the room before it centered on the jury. They were there after the venue had to be changed three times to make sure the women were put in prison.

"Hello, ladies and gentlemen."

As his mother was told to shut up several times, he was asked questions by the state-appointed attorney for his mother. The man looked like he'd gone a couple of rounds with someone bigger than him. Wats knew that the day before yesterday, he'd been caught unawares, and Christa, Booker's mother, had knocked him around before the prison guards had gotten their Tasers out and used them on her. No amount of begging to the judge had been able to get the man out of being their attorney after that. No one, he had heard, wanted anything to do with the Bitches Four, as they'd been calling them at home.

"When you were living at home, did your mother provide you with food, money, and any of the essentials one would expect?" Wats had been told to only answer the question with yes or no if he could, but no babbling about things. So he told the man no. "Your mother didn't make sure you were fed? That you had clothing to wear? I find that hard to believe."

Since it wasn't a question, he didn't answer him. But Wats did begin to unbutton his shirt below the camera's view. This was something they all were going to do when called to the chair today. Show off how loving their mothers had been to them all.

"Mr. Wilkerson, what sort of relationship did you have with your mother? I'm sure that like all young men, you and your mother were very close. Some of the things that are coming out paint a picture of my client of her being something terrible, which is unlikely. Would you agree with that assessment?" He asked him which assessment he was referring to. "That your mother wasn't as terrible as the papers and others are making her out to be."

"Then yes, I would agree that the papers don't have it right about my mother. She was much worse than any of them can even fathom." He heard his mother and aunts start screaming how they were going to get him when they were free. It took another ten minutes to get them under control. "As for my relationship with her? I had none. I was there for window dressing, and that's all."

"She loved you, correct?" He heard someone snicker, and he smiled at that. It was his aunt that was making noises. He told the attorney he didn't think his mother loved anything or anyone. "That is a bold statement. Love between a mother and child is something that is cherished."

Wats wasn't sure why the attorney was going on about his and his mother's relationship. He wondered why he wasn't talking about how his mother had plotted with the rest of them in killing his Aunt Holly. Or how they made it impossible for her and everyone else around them to live without fear. Even to ask about the deaths they'd caused and written about in their daily diaries. When he looked over at North, he told him it was time to bare it all.

"My mother was a manipulative bitch that should never have had children. Actually, she tried not to have them, right up until she needed one. Tina would beat me, yes, beat me or have someone else do it with a whip right up until she was arrested and put in jail." Standing up, he pulled his shirt off over his head, not bothering with the other buttons, and showed the jury his back. "This is how my mother got what she wanted. Do you see these scars? They're from a lifetime of being cornered about grades, the women I dated, or my hanging out with my cousin when she disapproved of him. And when I got too big for her to beat on her own, she hired people to do it for her. Ribs, arms, and legs were beaten so badly I can't stand to have anything touch me there. The last time she had someone beating me was when I, at the age of twenty-nine, decided I'd had enough dancing around her and that my life was just that — my life. She didn't like that, as you can see."

"You mother fucker. I should have aborted you right along with all the other creatures I got caught with. But we had to do better than Holly." He could hear someone telling her to shut up — it sounded to him like it was Penny. "I will not shut up. This is my time to tell the world that I wanted the best, and I, by God, got it at all costs. No one tells me no and lives to do it again."

The sound of the gavel banging had him smiling. He could imagine the new judge trying to regain control of the women. Wats wondered not for the first time since this started if anyone would ever get control of his mother and aunts. When they didn't want to hear the answers you gave them about something, they simply pretended you didn't say a word. His uncle Clayton had figured that out when visiting the jail they were being held in.

A break was called to take the women back to their cells. He was asked, politely, to return in an hour, and he said he'd be there so long as he didn't have an emergency. They'd approved him being able to leave when he'd been summoned here today, as he had a practice. The judge, he'd forgotten his name, looked like he was ready to call it a day even though it was only nine-thirty in the morning.

"Did you hear about the trial for Fran and Phoenix? Well, Fran's trial anyway." Wats said to Booker that he'd not as he dug into his breakfast. He'd not been able to eat before leaving the house this morning. "The judge has decided that since the two of them were together when Phoenix shot the judge, he's going to have them both judged in federal court. They're being taken away in the morning. I think that will make Amy sleep better at night. There is no way they'll be able to cover that up. Judge Wessex was well respected, even by those that she sent away. Because she was fair to everyone."

Lorinda Wessex had been murdered when

Amy's sister, Phoenix, had pulled a gun from one of the officers trying to untangle a fight in the courtroom several weeks ago. Wats had done all he could for her while in the courtroom, but she passed a few days later from it. Her daughter Charlie was just like her mom.

After breakfast, they sat around the restaurant and talked. They had been getting together with their dads at least once a week since their mothers had been arrested. Wats had been staying with his dad for the last few weeks since his condo was being used by Rayne and her grandda James. They'd be moving out soon, he realized, as the house that was being put on the land for James was nearly finished. The rest of them had even pitched in and made sure that the double wide, all that James wanted, was furnished as well.

"Are you listening to me?" He looked at Mars when he spoke. Smiling at him, he told him he'd been thinking about other things. "I can tell. You were thinking of Rayne again, weren't you?"

Looking around the table, he realized it was only him and Mars. Wats started to ask where the others had gone but didn't want to embarrass himself any more than he already had. Instead, he told him he was thinking about her.

"She's looking for a part-time job. Know of

any that she can work around her school schedule?" Wats asked him why he didn't hire her. "I thought you needed someone to answer phones and make appointments. That would be a good job for her, don't you think? Not too stressful, and she could work with you on her degree."

"She is studying to be a nurse. I might be able to hire her for that too when she's finished up." Mars said that was what he'd been thinking too. He also pointed out that he'd not answered his question. "I like her. Very much. I've been working up to asking her on a date. Don't tell the others."

"Why do you have to work up to it?" Wats explained it to him. "I can see where that might be an issue. You told her no strings until the house was finished when she moved into your condo. But that should be soon, right?"

"Yes. North said they were out today to inspect the place before they could hook it up to the power or water. I'm not sure which one, but you get it." Mars told him he understood as he stood up to go. "I need to talk to you about something. It's important to me, anyway. What would you do if you and I were to switch situations with my mother? I've been bothered by it for a few nights, and I'm kind of losing some sleep over it. She wants me to go there and speak to her. Actually, she would be speaking at me — that's the way it has always been with her. Mother wants me to get her an attorney that will get her out of prison. I don't want that. Ever."

"Then I think you have your answer. As for going to see her, do you remember how she spoke to you this morning? How she told you she was gunning for you when she got out? Not that she is ever getting out, but you do remember that, don't you?" Wats said he did. "What more would you say to her if you were face to face that you need to say to her? Anything at all? I'm not telling you not to go. I'm just pointing out a few things for you to think about if you do go."

"Closure? Tell her how much I dislike her? I don't know. Nothing comes to mind that I know she'll hear when I say it to her." Mars nodded and asked him again if he thought he had his answer. "I do. Thanks, buddy. I knew you'd be the one to tell me to go or not. I just needed to see if I was being — I don't know, stupid or something, thinking I had to go. Understand?"

"Yes. I believe it will take you some time to get over that feeling of having to do whatever you're told by them. I know it would for me as well."

Wats wondered if Aunt Holly had ever whipped Mars. She would have, he realized then, if she thought he needed it. But neither of them, he knew, would feel good about it. Her for having to do that, but Mars would have been devastated if she'd had to do it too. They all missed their aunt as much as Mars did his mom. She was mother to all of them.

"Now, I have a favor I need from you. I'd very much like to get something for the baby's room that will be his or hers forever. I know you've been around a lot of new families, but I want something so much better than that for my child and wife. If you could give that some thought, I'd be ever so grateful." He paused. "Also, something very nice for my wife. I would absolutely love to be able to show her how much I dearly love her."

"No spa or chocolate." Mars asked Wats why not. "I've heard that women, after having a baby, do not want you to think of them as fat or out of shape. That's what they think when you give them the spa. And like you said, everyone gives chocolates. I'd skip that too. You really need to start taking Abby out more. Think of it as pre-baby dates. Because after it comes, you're not going to have a lot of time for that sort of thing. At least that's what I'm to understand."

"I like that idea. Both of us have been working from home a lot, and it's getting to the point that when my phone rings, I dread it. Something else I have to make a decision on. It's wonderful having all this money, but I don't think anyone knows how much work it is to keep it coming in. I guess I could just live off the interest from everything, but that would really drive me nuts. Not knowing if there was going to be another income." He laughed with Mars. "I'm too much of a 'saving for a rainy day' sort of person. Also, I wanted to tell you that I'm opening the shop next week. I'm getting excited about that."

"I will be there daily for lunch." Mars told him he was hoping so. "Have you found someone to come in and serve your customers?"

"Yes. I hired a few high school kids to help out. Abby came up with the idea of telling them if they were to save at least twenty-five hundred dollars before they went to college, we'd match whatever they had saved up." Mars laughed. "I'm pretty sure we're going to meet it anyway, but it's nice to make them have to work for some of the cash."

"I like that idea. I thought for about ten seconds of hiring some high school kids that might be thinking about going into medicine, but I don't want to put any pressure on anyone. There are just too many drugs and information that they could easily get into. Not that I'd not trust someone, but kids and peer pressure can be terrible." Wats was surprised when he was told the bill had been paid. "I guess I owe someone lunch."

The courtroom was full, he could see as he made his way into the building. They were all in the same room, the cousins and their dads, in the sub-levels of the courthouse. The women on trial wouldn't know they were there and cause some trouble, and all of them felt much safer than they would if they had to be in the courtroom with them. They were all insane.

~*~

Rayne looked around the condo once again. It had been really nice staying here—she was going to miss it. Not that Grandda having a new place to live wasn't going to be great, but she knew this place. She also had liked the smell of the place.

It was silly, she knew, that she had washed up Wats's laundry and put it away for him, with the exception of one of his shirts. She'd been wearing it to bed nightly. Glancing at her bag of stuff that was going to the new place, Rayne wondered if he'd miss just one shirt. He did have a great deal of white shirts, she told herself. Then it occurred to her that he might just miss one of his shirts—she would. But she didn't have a lot of stuff in the first place.

As she was going to her bag, Wats and his brother came into the living room and announced that they were there to get them moved. Mars moved into the kitchen, and Rayne's face heated up when Wats smiled at her.

"You look like you've been caught at something bad." *He couldn't have said anything else, could he?* she thought. Her face heated up more, and he grinned at her just a little more. "Now I have to know what you've been up to. Did you rob me blind, my dear?"

"It was only a shirt. You'd never miss it. I can give it back, but it's been so comfy to sleep in. I'll give it back to you. After I wash it. Yes, after I— Why are you looking at me like that?" He asked her how he was looking at her, his voice deeper than before. There was also a cadence that she'd not noticed too until right now. "Like you're going to taste me. Or something."

"I want to. Right now, I want nothing more than to ask you to put on my shirt and nothing else and let me taste you." Her body warmed, her lips felt dry. Licking them, giving them just a little moisture had Wats groaning deeply in his throat. "I've been thinking about you a great deal, Rayne. Not sexually — not until now — but how it would feel to kiss you. To take you on a date and have some— Would you go out with me?"

"Yes." When Wats turned from her and looked

in the doorway, she did as well. It was difficult, she thought, to pull her glance from the man. When he asked his cousin what he wanted, the laughter set off her temper, and she found herself standing in front of the big man poking him in the chest. "What did you want that was so important that you had to interrupt our conversation? Was it that important?"

"No, not really." He laughed again. "Wats, I like her. She's a keeper. If I'm right on this, and I think I am, she'll fit right in with the rest of the group. I was just asking Wats here if he wanted to get some lunch on the way over to the new place. I missed my breakfast, and he's had me running him around all morning."

"Oh." Again her face heated up, and she felt herself feeling stupid and awkward. Instead of letting her mouth get herself into more trouble, she looked at Wats again. "I'm not sure what's going on here. I don't have any idea why I want you to take me into your arms and make me feel like I'm something special. I've never felt that way with anyone before. I don't know you well enough to have those feelings for you. I just find myself feeling stupid all the time."

Instead of telling her she *was* being stupid, Wats pulled her into his arms and held her tightly. Every insecurity she had about herself, all the doubts that anyone would or could love her, seemed to just melt away. Closing her eyes against all the emotions that were pinging all over her mind and body, Rayne just let herself enjoy being held. It might well never happen for her again.

"I've been thinking that you could come and work for me. Answer the phone, let me help you with your education into becoming a nurse. But right now, all I can think about is chasing you around my office and having my way with you." She pulled back enough to look up at him. "We'd never get anything accomplished, I'm afraid."

"This is really strange for me." He said it was for him as well. "I haven't dated all that much. Rarely a second one if I do go out with someone. I'm probably the world's oldest virgin at twenty-six."

He laughed. It didn't feel like he was making fun of her, nor did he tell her that her being a virgin was shocking to him. No, it felt like he was laughing because he was enjoying himself. Smiling at him, she asked him if he was as loony as he seemed.

"More than likely, I think. But I would love for you to come by my offices and see if you could perhaps work for me. I don't have a great many patients as yet. Just enough to keep me on my toes. I seem to take care of the family injuries more than I do anyone coming into the offices." She asked him about the filing. "I do have a sort of system in mind, but if you could figure out something, I'd be glad to have it. I just came from a large practice with about a dozen other doctors and nurses, and this part is all new for me."

He picked up her bags when Mars asked him from the other room if they were ready. She took the smaller bag that was her grandda's and took it out to the truck too. There, sitting in the driveway, was a brand new car. It even had a large bow on it. She dropped everything and wanted to get a closer look at it.

"North bought it for you and your grandda. He said he noticed that you didn't have a very reliable vehicle, and he didn't want to make you unable to go to class or take James to the doctor — us, I would guess — if your car didn't start." She told Mars that was just too much. "Not to him, it's not. He feels terrible that you had to live in that other house. I do as well. Someone should have fixed it for you rather than just blowing you off when you needed at least a new furnace. Those are necessities, and the bank should have made sure they were in good working order."

"I'll be ever so careful with it. And I won't put any more miles on it than necessary." Wats asked her why she thought she had to not put miles on it.

"I don't know. To resell it, I suppose."

"I'm sure he means for you to use it as much as you want. There isn't any reason that he'd not want you to be doing that." Wats kissed her on the mouth as he handed her the car keys. "You drive it over to the new house to see if it's something you can get used to. It has a full tank of gas, and there is a standing order at the local gas stations for you to fill it up whenever you need to." She started to complain that it was too much. "Before you say something like you're not going to do that, it's not just for you, Rayne, but for your grandda as well. We've all gone to college, so we know how tight things can be when you're trying to get an education. Just think of this as we're helping you graduate without any worries."

It was too much. Not just the car and the house, but her feelings for Wats. Instead of saying something else about it all, she got into the car and waited for them to do the same. Rayne's emotions were too new, too everything right now, and she didn't want to do or say something that she might well regret later.

Grandda rode over to the house with her. He was playing around with the glove box, he called it, and the dials on the radio. When they were coming up on the pharmacy, he remembered he had a prescription to pick up. Wondering how she was going to afford that and pay for her late book fees, she went inside while Grandda told Mars what they were doing. Waiting in line, she thought of all the things she still needed to finish up before the end of term.

This was her last term in college. It was so close that she could almost taste it. Of course, she still would have to take her state boards, but she'd been studying for that since the beginning and hoped that she'd not have any trouble with it. Three more weeks of classes, and she'd be ready to sit in a room with other nurses to be and take the test. Christ, it had been a long road, but she was so happy that she'd been able to finish it in a reasonable amount of time.

It was her turn next in the line.

"Hello, Rayne. How's the new home? I bet your grandda is loving all the rooms on one floor." She told the pharmacist they were headed out there now to see it. "I got a call from Wats. He said you were going to be working for him in the office. He couldn't get a better nurse to work with him. How much longer do you have to go, honey?"

Mr. Windle handed her the bag with her grandda's prescription in it as she told him how long she had to go. He asked her if working with him over the summer had gotten her the credits she'd needed last year.

"Yes. They were impressed with how much you were able to help me with. And when I took my test on pharmacology, I aced it." She looked for the price on the bag and couldn't find it. "I don't know how much I'm going to need to pay. I mean, I know Brenda will need to ring me out, and I don't want to cause her any undue trouble."

"No charge." She asked him what he meant. "Wats is a good man and a great doctor. He's also helping my daughter out with her summer camp needs. I know you've met my daughter. She is going to a special ed camp this summer and spring that Wats was able to get her into. I owe that man more than I can ever repay him. I don't charge them for any meds they need, and since you're going to be working for him, I don't want to charge you either. Call it a perk."

"But I know that Grandda's meds are expensive, Mr. Windle. That's too much for someone that hasn't even worked yet."

He told her it wasn't to him. Nor for what the Wilkersons, the younger generation anyway, had done for him and his family. She didn't know what to say, so Rayne thanked him profusely for the perk and made her way out to the car.

Grandda was talking to Wesley Wilkerson, father to Wats, just as she came out of the pharmacy. She was unsure how she felt right now and had to have her grandda repeat with he'd just asked her. Mr. Wilkerson got into the backseat of the car and told her it was all right. He'd just hitch a ride over to the restaurant with her.

Rayne had always been a very careful driver. But having a car that not only stopped when you pushed on the brakes just a little but would leap forward when the gas pedal was engaged made her a nervous wreck. Neither of the men said a word to her when she started out with a jump and stopped hard enough to nearly toss them out of their seats. She'd never been so happy to pull into a parking lot as she was when she got to the place to meet the others for lunch. Grandda went in, but Mr. Wilkerson stayed behind with her.

"You all right, honey?" She said she was just a little on the nervous side. "I spoke to Wats just now. He invited me to meet you. He said that you and he were going to be seeing each other. I don't know how much you know about the wives of the family, but we're trying very hard to get to know our sons. I won't be intruding, will I?"

"Goodness no. I'm not sure of a lot of stuff going on right now." She told him everything, including the need to have Wats hold her and the prescription perk. "It's too much. And this car? While I really appreciate it, I'm sure it wasn't cheap. Not on top of them putting in a home for my grandda."

"You know my family, don't you? I mean, the fact that we're wealthy in our own right. Not to be rude, but I know that buying this car for you and putting in a better house for your grandfather isn't going to hurt them at all. They've been good boys all their lives—no thanks at all to myself and their parents, but because of my sister. You let them do this for you, Rayne. Please. If it worries you too much thinking that they want something else from you, then you'd be wrong. They all just see something they can fix, and they do it. I'm very proud of them for that."

She turned and looked at the man. "When I was ten years old, I saw your wife berating Wats for helping my grandma to her car when it was snowing. He'd gone out and started it for her so that it would be warmed up when she got out there." Mr. Wilkerson said it sounded like something he'd do. "Not only did Tina slap him, but she kicked him when he slipped and fell on the ice. I hurt for him then. But you know what? The very next day, he did the same thing, helping another person out to their car that he'd warmed up for her as well. I think a part of me fell in love with Wats that day. Not just for helping out two women that he more than likely didn't know all that well, but because he didn't not do it even after being hurt and humiliated by his own mother." Rayne wiped at a tear that had fallen. "I'm sorry. I have no idea why I told you that. You must think I'm a ninny."

"Ninny? You've been hanging out with your grandda too much, I think. But no, Rayne, I think you telling me that was something you needed to do. And believe it or not, I needed to hear it. Not for Tina, but knowing that my son was a great deal stronger than I was when it came to his mother. Thank you for that. Now, let's go and have some lunch and have a little bit of fun."

They did have fun. The meal was loud, and laughter rang out throughout the place. When the others, the other cousins, joined them, it was even louder, with more laughter going around. When Wats took her hand under the table, Rayne felt wonderful, like she was a part of something grand, and she was going to enjoy it as much as she could. Wats liked her, she thought, and she liked him as well. This was turning out to be a much better day than she'd thought it would be when she'd gotten up today.

Chapter 2

Tina wanted to talk to someone about her being able to get home. There was absolutely no reason for her to be locked up like this. Didn't they understand that they were keeping her from doing her civic duties? Now that she was going to be in charge of things, she needed to make it known that she was nothing like Eita was, bless her heart. But Tina was going to be hard on the people in this subhuman town. The officer that brought her a tray for her lunch wouldn't speak to her anymore, but that didn't stop Tina from making her demands known to the woman.

"Did you call my husband and tell him I want him down here? Don't just stand there, answer me, damn it. I have to speak to him about this rumor I heard about that bastard son of Holly's moving into my home." The woman didn't speak to her, but she did give her that knowing smile. "You're an idiot. I hope someone figures that out before you get someone killed. It wouldn't be too bad if you were killed, but I'm thinking with the way my luck has been going, I'll be hurt as well. Get me a phone, and I'll make the call myself. I've been in this place for far too long, and I want my things."

"If you have any complaints, you need to put them in writing and turn them into the mayor. I don't think it will do you much good, however, since the mayor we have is lazier than you are. However, in a few weeks, about twelve days, I think, we're having another vote, and there will be a new mayor in town." The woman laughed. "Though I doubt very much that will do you any good either since Clayton Wilkerson is going to be a shoo-in for the position."

"There is no way he's going to be running for anything. Christ, his wife has only been gone for a few weeks, and he's out running around like he doesn't have a clue? I tell you, if not for their wives, there is no telling what sort of shit they'd be getting up to. I'll have to have a conversation with him as well. I want to set him straight on that and a few other things I have on my mind. Why are you still standing here? Don't you listen? Get me a phone.

Now, damn it." Putting out her hand, she tapped her foot. That was all it would take for most of the town to do what she wanted before. There was no reason for her to think it wasn't going to work on this dumbass. But she still stood there like she'd not spoken a single word to her. "I'm sick to death of the way I'm being treated in here. I want you to go find me someone that will answer my questions and do what I tell them to do. This is fucking stupid. And you're going to get it when I finally get out of this nasty place."

"Are you threatening me?" Tina knew better than to answer that question. A few days ago, one of the people down the hall from her had said she was threatening the officer and had gotten charged with something like threatening a person with a law degree or some other shit. "I'm not going to bring you a phone. You're not going to get out of here until you move to a larger prison. Which can't be soon enough for those of us that have to be around you and the others. There isn't going to be any talking to your husband or any of the other men anymore, as they told us not to put calls through from you women. It's not a rumor that Mars and his lovely wife are moving into the mansion—it's a fact. They're going to have a baby as well. And I'm enjoying this more than I should, but there isn't anything you can do about it either. So, if there is nothing else I can do for you — not that I want to — but if there is nothing else, I'm going to go back to work."

"Listen here, you fucking bitch. Do you have any idea how much power I wield? How much money I have? It's more than you'll see in several lifetimes. I'm a Wilkerson, and because of me and the other women, it's a name that ensures whatever we want, we get. Even if we have to resort to making a few heads roll." The woman laughed. "Damn you, you fucking cunt. Get me, my husband. He'll have you fired so quickly you won't be able to — Where the hell are you going? You don't turn your back to me. Get your ass back here until I tell you I'm finished talking to you. Damn it."

The woman was laughing all the way down the hall. Tina couldn't see who was in the other cells, but she did know some of them held the others that had been arrested that day. When the bitch came back, a cell phone in her hands, Tina felt like she'd won this battle, but she only held it out just far enough that she wasn't able to reach it.

"By the way, I don't know if you were told this or not, but your son is married now. A very nice woman too. Her name is Amy." Tina couldn't even fathom why this woman would tell her such an outrageous lie. She asked her about it. "No reason for me to lie to you about it. But I think they're trying to have a baby too. That would make you a grandma. Ha. That's funny. You a grandma."

"No fucking way is that going to happen. I need to speak to him before, God forbid, he actually does get this woman knocked up. He doesn't understand that with money comes hookers and streetwalkers wanting to take every penny he has. I'll just have to teach him a few lessons in that. Christ. She's not going to be married to my son nor anyone else when I'm finished with her." Tina was already plotting ways to end the other woman's life. "I'll need her name and schedule she keeps. I'm sure, like all money-grubbing fucking bitches, she's thinking she's going to get his money. He should know by now that I'll say when and who he's going to marry. And if you call me a grandmother once more, I will kill you."

Again, the stupid cow walked away with laughter ringing around the hall. It seemed to be twice as loud as it usually was. The worst part was that she kept singing about how they were going to grandma's house. She knew it was a kid's song, but it was making her crazy. Screaming, just letting off some steam that she'd not been able to since being brought here, Tina sat down on the bed.

Too much right now. Mentally sorting through the things that had been told her, Tina put them in order of importance. To her, it was all important, but as she had learned from Eita, if you ran around doing a lot of things at once, it was difficult to bask in the wonderful moments when you were able to finish one of the projects. Eita was a pro at being a Wilkerson. Tina wished every day that the bullet that had ended the life of her best friend in the world had taken out Crista, who had killed Eita. Sure, she'd not be in charge right now, but Eita was the best at getting things done. She would have had them all out of here by now, and they would be on the way to getting things back the way they were. When they were in charge.

"It's all that woman's fault." Holly had been killed by them, and the fact that she was making their lives so fucking difficult from the grave pissed Tina off so much she wanted to go and dig her up and kill her all over again. "She wasn't worth the spit of cum that created her if you were to ask me."

Since she couldn't get on the party line that they'd had, nor talk face to face with any of the other women, she had to talk to herself. Tina didn't mind her own company, but long stretches of no one to speak to really depressed her. Who was there for her when she came up with one of her many brilliant ideas? No one.

They wouldn't allow her to have another pen to keep notes with because she'd tried to use it to pick the lock. If some low-brow mouth breather had been in the cage with her, she would have made them break her out. Tina was also grateful that she wasn't with a low life. Shivering, she looked around her cage.

To call it a cell wasn't fair. It was a cage, something to hold someone in. She'd been in jail a couple of times in her youth, but never for this long. All she'd had to do was make a phone call to her mother or her father, and they'd send someone out to get her. Then they paid off the other person, the reason she'd been arrested, but it never showed up on her record. Having wealthy parents had been a wonderful thing. But sadly, she'd had to kill them when they started making noises of cutting her off from their fortune.

"Didn't I get the shaft on that too? The only mention of me was to tell me that no matter what happened to my brother, I still didn't get to inherit any of their money. Fuckers. Still killed him, now didn't I? If I couldn't have it, neither could he."

Laughing at herself, she sat down on the only seat in the cage. Her cot, they called it. Not the floor. The fucking place only got cleaned three times a week, and never on the weekend. She could still see some of the bits of food that she'd dropped on the floor the night before last. Whoever thought that having a single sandwich on plain white bread could constitute a meal was out of their ever-loving mind.

Also, she hated to admit it, but she thought she was putting on weight. She'd been a size four most all of her life. Even when she'd been fat with Watson, she'd managed to not put on any more than five pounds. Of course, the doctor was pissy about that, telling her that she'd hurt her child. Like she gave a shit about him. The only reason any of them stayed pregnant was because Holly, the cunt, had had a son. Not that anyone considered her to be a part of the family, but Eita said it would look good on them to not just have a child for their inheritance but to have a son. It had taken her five abortions before she'd gotten a son. Fuck, that had been the worst part, having to have sex with Wesley so much to make one. She shivered again like someone had walked over her grave.

"Probably Holly."

Laughing at her own joke, she looked up to see a man standing there. While she had no idea who he was, she tried to make herself look better and thinner by sucking in her cheeks and throwing her shoulders back to make her breasts look good. For all the money she'd put out for them, or Wesley had, she wanted everyone to see how nice they were.

"Not on your life. I'm here to tell you, Christina Wilson, that you've been found guilty of five counts of murder in the first degree. Three counts of murder in the second degree, and—"

"What the fuck are you talking about? I'm getting out of here. And my name is Wilkerson, not Wilson. That name is meaningless to me." He said she wasn't, actually. "Oh yes, I am. I will be living in the big house. There wasn't even a trial. You can't convict someone without a trial."

"The trial was conducted over the last three days. It ended an hour ago with the jury finding you all guilty of the same crimes. You weren't there because, as the judge stated, you weren't cooperating and were causing a ruckus, so you would have to learn your verdict this way. Since you and the other women wanted to be tried as one, then you all got the same sentencing. Each murder committed by you or any of the other women is counted against each of you. I know for a fact that you were told this would happen if you did things this way." She said she wanted to change her mind. "It's not going to work either. The paperwork has been filed, and now you only have to wait on your sentencing. In the meantime, you'll be sent, with the others, to prison. A larger building than this one that won't stand for the way you've treated the people that work here."

"First of all, I'm not happy with this so-called verdict that you've given me. It's a lie. I won't have it." The man smiled at her. "Secondly, the only place I'm going is home. Where my husband had better be fixing it back the way I wanted it before all this mess was put upon us. I mean, what did I do, really? Nothing that anyone else in my position wouldn't do if they were a Wilkerson with all the money in the world. You go tell that judge to— Better yet, you tell him to get his ass down here and let me talk to him. I cannot believe he expects me to just be all right with this shit. Go and get him."

"No." She asked him what he'd said to her. "I said no. I know it's not a word you might be familiar with, but I'm not going to do anything for you. As far as I'm concerned, you needed to be put in prison a long time ago. Now, I've told you, and you seem to understand what is happening. I'm going to tell the others—"

"I *do not* understand what is happening, you fucking moron. I want to know why no one is coming here to get me out of this fucking place. There is no way that a jury of my peers would have the balls to put me in a place so far from my home. However will I be able to go to my clubs and have lunch with the others? No, I don't understand, and you're not leaving here until you understand that I'm not in any way going anyplace that isn't the Wilkerson Mansion. Do you fucking hear me?"

He walked away. Just walked away from her like she wasn't still speaking to him. She wished now that she'd gotten his name. There was going to be hell to pay when she was free from here. Mother fucker. Who in their right mind would send her, Tina Wilkerson, off to prison for the lame assed things they were blaming her for?

She heard one of the other women screaming — Tina thought it was Christa. Now there was a person that deserved to go to prison. Killing Eita had been what had started all this. She just had to take out her gun and fire it when everyone knew that Eita had it all under control.

"The first thing I'm going to do when I get out of here is to make sure she's no longer welcome around us. For a time, anyway. We'll have a discussion. But since I'm married to the oldest son, I get to decide. Everyone knows the one in charge is the one the married to the oldest." She thought about that for a moment and smiled. "New rules, bitches. Just wait and see."

She was told she needed to get her things together about an hour later. Who really knew what time it was. There were no clocks that she could see. Nothing to tell her what time it was other than the shitty meals she was brought. Getting things gathered up, she was glad she didn't have anyone bring too much in for her to use. Putting it in the duffle they'd handed her would have crumbled it all up.

Tina was standing at the door when a man in a suit, along with the man who had been by earlier, approached.

"Christina Wilson, you've been—" She said it was Tina Wilkerson. "No. According to the divorce paperwork I was handed when I came to fetch you, you're no longer entitled to use the name Wilkerson for personal use nor in business dealings. In the event that your ex-husband wants to remarry."

"Remarry? Honey, I don't know how you came to that conclusion that he could remarry, but he's married to me. Until death, we do part, which will be sooner than he expects the way things are going this minute. Now get out of my way so I can go home. You've no idea how excited I am right now." He laughed with her as he chained her up. "I suppose you think this is necessary? I'm only going out to the limo that I'm sure Wesley sent for me.

Really? You have to show how powerful you are now? "Christ, I hate fucking men."

"Not from what I heard, you don't." She didn't know what that meant but let it go. She saw the others in her click standing in the big hall too. They all had the same duffle and looked as excited as she did. "All right. We're going to load up in the vans out front. Then you will—"

"Where is Christa? I have a few things to say to her." The officer at the door asked her if she'd heard yet. "Heard what? Where is Christa Wilkerson? I need to see her too. We're the best group of women that—"

"Christa committed suicide two nights ago."

Chapter 3

Wats found Booker sitting outside the house that had been on the market. He had been sitting out here, the realtor told him since they'd arrived. Sitting down next to his cousin, he sat there in silence, waiting on Booker to say something first. It didn't take him long to speak up.

"I don't like me right now." Wats asked him what he meant by that. "Is a son supposed to feel relieved that his mother is gone? That she's no longer a threat to me or those that I love? I doubt very much anyone feels like this when their mother chews her wrists open rather than go on for another day. She left me a note. Did I tell you?"

"I heard, but I didn't hear what it said." Booker handed him the note. It was still sealed. "You've not read it yet. Is there a reason for that?"

"I can't. I know it's going to be something along the lines that it's all my fault that she's done this. Or Dad's. Did I tell you that Dad and I are planning a trip to go ice fishing this winter? I've never done it before. I'm actually looking forward to it." Wats was planning trips with his dad as well. More along the lines of baseball games and camping trips. "Will you read it for me? Not to me, but just read it, then if it's not too overwhelming, I'll take it."

"All right. But what happens if it's all drivel about you causing her demise? I'm reasonably sure she isn't going to be any different with this than any of the rest of them have been." Wats laughed. "Later, sometime soon, you'll have to look at the recording of the women being sent to the prison. It made my entire day just watching the looks on their faces when they realized they weren't going home, but to a larger facility." He thought about what he'd said. "I'm sorry. Booker. That was really insensitive of me."

"No. I would love to watch it. As I said, I have no feeling whatsoever about my mother. I don't think I have for a very long time." The door opened behind them, and the realtor asked if Booker wanted to see any more of the house. "No. I've seen enough. Tell the bank, who I know owns this place, that I'll give them fifty cents on the dollar for what is owed in back taxes and nothing more. The house has been on the market for far too long for someone to pay what they're asking. Also, they'll give me a short-term loan for the balance, or I'll pay cash for the house, and they'll not earn anything from the deal." He looked at Wats before continuing with the woman making notes. "Also, this is a deal-breaker—I want a good deal on the surrounding acreage. I looked it up—it's nearly three hundred acres, not including the fifty around the house."

"I don't think they'll go for that, Mr. Wilkerson." Booker told her he'd just find another house and another realtor. "All right. I'll see what I can do."

Wats could tell that Booker had pissed the woman off. And when she went into the house again, he asked him why he'd do that. She'd not done anything wrong that he'd seen. Booker said she'd commented that the house had several more offers on it, all of them higher than the asking price.

"She lied to you." He nodded. "I think people hear that you're a college professor and a chemistry one at that and automatically think you're a nerd and know nothing about anything other than a lab. But what they don't realize, until it's too late, is that not only are you brilliant, but you also have a good sense of the market."

"Yeah, that's what gets people in trouble. Assuming." He asked him to open the letter. "I've decided that I want you to read it to me, buddy. I want to feel like—I don't know. I need to feel something about my mother instead of just this nothing void that I have about her now. Hate and love, they're two sides of the same coin if you're not careful."

Wats opened the envelope, and something fell out. Picking up the napkin that was covered in blood, he put it on his lap and read a few lines to himself before turning to Booker. He asked him if he was sure he wanted to hear it.

"Yes. Now that I know by the look on your face that it's as bad as I thought it would be. Go ahead. I'm assuming that's my mother's blood. Go on, Wats. I won't hold it against you for what the bitch said to me." Booker grinned. "Go on, buddy. Read it to me."

"*Dear worthless piece of shit.*" He looked at Booker when he laughed. "*I'm dead now, and it's all your fault. Your father's too, but he will have to wonder for the rest of his life why I have come to despise him so much. I'm willing to bet that he will never date again because he'll come to realize that I was the best thing ever for him. I hope he fails as much as I know you will.*"

"She certainly has a very high opinion of herself, don't you think?" They both laughed, and it felt good. "Believe it or not, Dad just asked me yesterday if I had a problem with him dating. I told him hell no, to go for it. I think like the others, my dad has been lonely for a very long time."

"I agree with you there. I know my dad is having a blast helping Uncle Clayton run for mayor. I think between the two of them, they'll get this town back on track." He glanced at the letter again. "Are you ready for more?" Booker nodded. *"I'm going to kill myself. Not because I feel guilty about anything I've done. I do regret killing Eita. My heart does ache so badly for what I did to her. She would have taken us all as far as the White House if she'd been alive. No, I'm taking my own life because I want you to think about it for the rest of your life. How you, my only son, treated me so badly when I needed you most. Actually, all your life you have been such a terrible person. I hope to God you fail at every turn. That you never marry — not that anyone would have you, but I want you to fail at that as well. The marriage your father and I had was perfect, but you never took the time to learn from me — you ungrateful bastard. I wish every day that I had aborted you along with the other unwanted trash that I had and remained a childless woman. I know I would have enjoyed my life so much more without you in it. You're to take this napkin that I had to steal from the jail that you left me in and keep it on your person for the rest of your days. I want you to think about what you've done to me, your own mother, every time you see it.* Then she signs it with her name. What do you want to do with this?"

"I'm going to burn it with the napkin." He stood up just as the door was opening behind them again. The realtor said the bank wished to speak to him. "I'm a very busy man, Ms. James. If he's not willing to come to my terms, then I'm sorry, I really am, but I'm not going to dick around when I know for a fact that there are several other houses on the market that I can get for a good deal less than the asking price. This is a buyers' market right now, and I intend to get as much bang for my buck as I can."

"Mr. Waller said that if you pay off the back taxes, he'll throw in the land, as it has no access other than the land around this house. No one wants to buy it, and the house when all they want to do is plant some corn." She smiled at him. "I told him you were going to walk away from this deal over a few bucks that he would be able to write off at the end of the year. Is that all right?"

"Yes. And you figure out what your commissions would have been for the asking price of the house, and I'll gladly pay that to you." She told him that was nice but not necessary. "No, it's not, but that's the way I work. You went to bat for me, even though you lied to me about the other offers, and I appreciate that."

"I'm sorry, sir. That's what I was told to tell you." He told her she'd more than likely sell more houses if she was honest with people. "I might just do that from now on. I really don't care for lying to people that are spending that much money for a home they might just hate because of me. Thank you, sir. Very much."

"Anytime." Booker looked at him. "I have to head to the bank, I'm sure, so why don't the two of us have some lunch, then see what sort of trouble we can get into? I heard through Abby that you're dating Rayne. I like her. We've been friends for a very long time. I don't want to threaten you or anything, but please don't hurt her."

"I don't plan on it. She is going to my home today to see if she can stand to live there. Not that I don't think she'll love it as much as I do, but that would be up to her where we live. If this goes that far. I'm not sure what we're doing right now, to be honest. I've spoken to North about her grandda coming to live with us and leaving the house he just put in empty. He told me it didn't matter to him one way or the other, he'd just find himself a renter, and that would be all right too." Booker said he might use it if North doesn't hire someone to watch over the fields he just purchased. "You're right. I never realized this land would butt up against his. That's wonderful. Also, you might not have known this, but you also have access to the river from your place. I remember seeing a dock there when we were looking for mushrooms this past spring."

"It's hard to believe that so much has changed since then. None of it — well, hardly any of it — seems all that good, don't you agree? Aunt Holly was alive. We were all hanging out around the house. I don't care for mushrooms at all much. However, I certainly enjoyed going with you guys and her to find them. Her just being there when we needed her. Abby is filling in nicely for her, but I do miss her hugs. Aunt Holly had the best hugs. That was the best time. Don't you think?"

"Yes. I miss so much with her being gone. But Amy did tell me she's planning on organizing repeats of some of the things that she used to do with us. To keep her memory alive. I think that's a good idea." Booker agreed and then asked him if he wanted to walk through the house with him. "I do. But I would like for you to tell me what brought you outside in the first place. The lady showing you around, she called me when you'd been out here for so long."

"It hit me." Wats knew what he meant without him explaining too much. "She's gone. My mother is gone. All the aunts and their meanness are gone. It's all gone, and it hit me right in the heart so badly I needed to sit down."

"Nothing more than that? I worry about you sometimes. All of us, as a matter of fact. Especially after North telling us about his episode." Booker told him it was nothing like that. "I hope so. I can't lose another person in my life, Booker. It's too much now. I need you guys here to balance me out."

"I thought you had a girlfriend for that." He patted him on the back as they moved through the house he'd purchased. "As I said, I like Rayne. She's wonderful. Sheesh, Wats, I just bought a house. I wonder what dear old Mom is thinking about that."

They were both laughing as they made their way through the home. It was a nice place, but as he'd said to the realtor, it needed work after being empty for so long. The kitchen, while in good condition, was out of date and needed to be taken down to the studs and built again. Bringing it up to this decade.

There were six bedrooms on the second floor with ample closets and two bathrooms, one at each end of the long hallway. The master suite was on the third floor, and it looked to Wats like a person could simply live up there and never leave.

"The views from here are amazing. You can see deep into the woods from here and the river too." Booker opened up one of the doors, both of them thinking it was a closet. "Christ, it's a nursery. It's as big as my flipping condo. I love this place."

So did Wats. As they went to the bank to sign the paperwork, they had fun. He was glad that Booker was over whatever had happened at the house and was moving on. Now, if he could only convince Brandon of the same thing. The man wasn't in a funk—the opposite, as a matter of fact. But Wats was more worried about him than he was any of the rest of them.

Chapter 4

Rayne waited for her turn to talk to her adviser. She'd been called in, along with the rest of the nursing students that were in their home stretch. After four and a half long years of being together, they were as close as they could be to each other. And none of them seemed to have any idea what this was about. When her name was called, she got high fives from the others still waiting as she made her way into the office.

"Hello, Rayne. I'm sorry about this short notice, but there are some things we'd like to speak to you and the others about. As you might have heard, there has been a shake-up at the hospital." She said she'd not heard anything. "I'm sorry. Then let me explain. I was hoping we could get behind this before it got out. The hospital is approximately fourteen nurses short now for staffing. I know that doesn't sound like a big deal, but I'm afraid it is. The inspector, who came by yesterday, said we cannot continue to have our doors open being so short-staffed as we have in the past. Since we're growing, the town, I mean, then we need to have the place up to staffing requirements at all times. He heard about the accident that put us in a bind a couple of months ago. The accident that was out on Highway Forty. Do you remember that?"

"I'm not from around here, sir. I drove back and forth from my home in Columbus for classes. I've only just moved here to go to the hospital for my technical courses. I like the small-town feeling here." He said that was why he'd called her in. "I don't understand."

"You and the other nursing students that have come in are being given an opportunity to take your state boards now. Today. From your grades, I believe you'd not have a bit of trouble passing. You've carried a good GPA since you started in this program." Her mind went all over the place about taking her tests today. "One of the other students decided she'd not have to stress about the test if she didn't have time to do so and is going to take hers now. I think that might be the case with you. You're not required to do this now, nor will it be held against you if you decide you want to wait. Because of you working in the hospital for us, even if you didn't want to go ahead and test, you'll be paid the wages of a nurse of your caliber. And you are a high-quality nurse, Ms. Oliver. The professors have enjoyed having you in their classes. The doctors that you worked with at the other hospital had nothing but rave reviews about your work ethic. I've not been able to say this to any of the others, nor will I to those that are still left, but I do believe you're going to pass this test without any trouble."

"Thank you." She sat there for a second. "I was going to be working for Doctor Wilkerson while I was going to school. Just answering the phone and such. May I call him and see if it would be all right with him if I were to go to the hospital instead?"

"Yes, by all means. Here, you use my phone, and I'll give you a few minutes." She felt like she was being rushed, and it didn't settle well with her belly or nerves. Taking a deep breath as soon as the door closed behind Mr. Elliot, she picked up the phone to call Wats. He was laughing when he answered her.

"Professor Elliot, I was just thinking—" She cut him off and told him that it was her, that she was in his office. "Is there something wrong? Are you hurt? Do you need me to come and get you?

Honey, what is it?"

"You're wonderful. I hope you know that. No, not a thing is wrong." She let the tears fall, another thing she did when she was stressed out. Cry. After telling him what she'd been told, she asked him about working for him. "You see, they're short-staffed. I don't think they want me there all the time, just until they can get some better trained nurses. I want to work with you. Very much so. I have visions of you chasing me around the desk. I'm getting off track here. I want to help you both, but I don't think that will do me a bit of good."

"Okay, just let my mind get out of the thought of you being naked on my desk for a moment." He didn't say anything for several seconds. "Not going to happen. So we might as well move on. Honey, do you want to do this today? I believe, like Professor Elliot, that you're going to do well at it. And the fact that you'll be finished with it all an entire eight weeks earlier would be one less stressful item off your list. Right?"

"Yes. I have been studying since I started. I think I could pass it, but how well, I have no idea. I want to do this, but I don't want to leave you in a situation that will make you short-staffed either." Wats told her he could find someone to work for him and that it was the desk part he was most looking forward to. "How about we do this then. I do this today, and then you move into the bedroom that I'm in, and we have this sexual tension taken care of once and for all?"

She knew he was still on the line. His breathing, harsh and quick, told her that. Rayne smiled when he asked for another minute, and she had to laugh when he said he needed to sit down. Telling him if he didn't want to do it they didn't have to was mean, she knew, but it got him talking again.

"Do you have any idea how many cold showers I've taken since I've met you? Several times a day, let me tell you." She giggled, a thing she'd not done since she was a child. "I agree to that, all of it. Take your test. I'll take you out to dinner tonight, then I will make love to you for the rest of the week. How's that for a plan?"

"I love it." She nearly told him she loved him as well but didn't want to make him feel as if he had to say it back to her. Instead, she told him she didn't know when she'd be home, but she'd let him know when she was finished. "I don't know what I'll do for lunch, but I'll figure something out. Wish me luck."

"Wishing you all the luck you'll need. However, I think you're going to do just fine. Let me know when you take your break, and I'll try to come and see you. I have a terrible need for a nice long kiss from you." She said he'd distract her. "Good point. I'll try very hard not to do that. All right, love. I'll look forward to seeing you soon."

Taking the National Council Licensure Examination, or NCLEX-RN for short, took six hours. That was all she was allotted anyway. She'd been told by other nursing personnel she'd worked with over the years that cramming for the exam wouldn't help. It was something you had to prepare for throughout your studies. That was exactly what she'd done. Even during the months she didn't have a heavy load, Rayne had gotten out her old notes and read over them to be ready. She'd been trying to get ready for this for a long time.

Being seated in a cubicle, Rayne could see that there were other people in the room with her. The proctor was there, and after he handed her the thick file for her to begin, he put her name on his chalkboard and the time she started. Opening it to the first page, Rayne closed it again and took in a deep breath, letting it out slowly. This was it, she told herself. What she'd worked for. Opening the file again, she started on the test.

"Ms. Oliver? You can take a break now if you'd like—it's been three hours." She looked around at the room. "You can take an hour if you wish. It won't count against you as timed testing unless you're late returning."

"Yes. I'd like that." He took her file, closed it, and put a piece of tape at every opening. After he signed his name to the strips of tape, she did as well. That way, when she returned, she'd know that no one tampered with her paperwork. Pulling out her phone, she called Wats. "I have less than an hour. I can't be late, he told me."

"I have ordered us some food, and all I need to do is bring it to you. I'm leaving here now." She asked if he had gotten her something to drink. She was very thirsty. "Yes. I noticed that you like sweet tea, so I had the deli make you a gallon that you can drink while we eat. I'm pulling up in front of the offices now if you want to come out."

Getting into the car, she laughed when he handed her a large picnic basket. As he drove down the block to the park area, he told her what he'd been doing since she'd called. Wats didn't ask her how she thought she was doing. Nor did he mention their plans for later. Just small talk that didn't put her on edge. In fact, it seemed to calm her in ways that she needed.

The subs were delicious, as was the tea. They talked about this and that. Wats told her how he was getting things ready for the addition he was putting on the back of his office. She asked him why he was expanding so soon.

"We're going to start hiring the construction company to work on the private school that we're building. I thought if we had a testing lab on site, as well as a place where workers can go for injuries that didn't require a hospital visit, we'd be one step closer to keeping everyone safe. Also, it's a good way not to overload the hospital emergency room." She told him what Elliot had told her. "I've noticed that too. With jobs coming in and all the other improvements being made around here, there are more homes being rented or bought up. Booker bought himself a home yesterday when I was with him."

"That's wonderful." Her phone buzzed, and she looked down at it. "That's odd. It's my aunt. I've not heard from her in years." Letting it go to voice mail, she smiled at Wats. "I think we need to discuss a few things. Going forward, I mean. I wanted to say this to you earlier, but I was chicken to do it. I'm falling in love with you, Wats. I know it's soon and all, but you're a wonderful person that simply makes me feel all warm and fuzzy inside. My heart is so full of happiness because of you. I sometimes have to pinch myself to make myself realize that I'm really with you. For however long you can stand me."

"I love you too." Her phone buzzed again. This time she didn't bother looking. "I think the moment I saw you, I was in love. You're nothing like I thought I wanted in someone to love, but so much better. I do love you, Rayne, and I cannot wait to spend time with you, getting to know everything there is to know about you."

He kissed her then. Pulling her to him, Wats made short work of the distance between them. They didn't paw at one another, as her aunts used to say about people dating, but the kiss made her hungrier for him than she'd been before. When they parted, it took several minutes for her breathing to even out. The alarm on her phone buzzed that she had twenty minutes to get back to the test.

"I'd better get back." She still had ten minutes after he pulled up in front of the building. "Thank you for this. I love that you didn't ask me about how I'd done. Or anything about the test. I didn't realize I didn't want you to do that until you didn't. You've relaxed me enough that I can go in and feel good about finishing up."

"I love you, Rayne." He kissed her again, but this one was quick. "Now, get in there and knock them dead, my dear. So I can take you out to dinner and then ravish you later."

She was laughing when she entered the room. The timer still had several minutes on it, but she didn't care. Getting her test back, signing off on the file again, she was refreshed and feeling good about herself as she dove into the rest of the questions.

~*~

Wats found his uncle just where he said he'd be. The others, his cousins as well as uncles and his dad, were already at the big house. Wats and Abby had put out some finger food, but he wasn't hungry just yet. The meeting had been called just before he'd gone to have lunch with Rayne. He didn't mention it to her because he wasn't sure if it would upset her. Sitting at the large dinner table, the others had already been served drinks, but he declined even that. For now, anyway. Uncle Clayton stood up.

"The prison called me earlier this morning to tell me they're having some trouble with the women. They want their husbands, all of us, to come up there and get them out, as you might well have guessed. However, the warden said he thought it was more than that. That their adjustment was difficult for them because they didn't have anything of their own with them. It took me a few minutes more of asking questions before I was able to figure it out. They just want out and aren't cooperating with anyone until they get it in their heads that where they are is a place they're going to be for a very long time." Wats asked if he thought they'd ever get that into their heads. "Doubtful, I think. They haven't so far. However, he wants me to go up there and try to explain to them that they're in prison for the rest of their days. The government is going to decide on their sentencing when their day comes up. The warden told me he believes, from the stuff he's been hearing, that they're going to be there until their deaths. They'll either get the death sentence or time without parole. Either one of those will not let them out."

"Why are you going?" Mars smiled at everyone at the table. "I'm not saying I should go. I'm thinking we all can understand how that would go. But why are you doing this again? Why don't we, as a group, go there and make them see reason? I'm not saying it will have any more effect than you going alone, Uncle Clayton, but there is safety in numbers. In this case, I'm thinking if we allow them to take their hatred out on all of us, it won't be so hard on a single person."

"I think he's right. This will give them a bigger focus on what they're wanting to say, and like Mars, I'm not sure it will do a bit of good." Wats looked around the room before continuing. "And while we're there, we should make sure that they understand completely that we're not going to drop everything we're doing to get our lives going to run up there and calm them down. It's almost as if they're still in charge of everything going on. They've made their beds, and they should have to figure out how to lie in them. Is the warden doing this because of who we are? Or does he really think we'll be able to help?"

"I didn't ask him." Uncle Clayton pulled out his cell phone and called the warden right then. He would never have done that before, gotten more information from someone before moving on. He was seeing lots of things that his dad and uncle had never done before that they did now. Uncle Clayton put his phone on the table and smiled. "He said you're right, Wats. The reason he is giving them this opportunity to get settled is because of us being Wilkersons and the fact that he didn't want to piss us off. I wouldn't have thought to ask that. So thanks, Wats. So now that we know the reason for him wanting me to go there, where should we go now?"

"The same way. All of us going up there and closing this once and for all. As you said, Mars, it's like we're still being ordered around by them." Dad looked over at him and smiled. "I think—and this is something you can do or not—but I'd think it would be a great idea for you boys in a relationship to take your ladies too. To sort of give them a little bit of how we're going on without them, and enjoying our lives so much better. I know that I am. I've been dating and having a blast."

"I have too, I must admit." All the uncles and his dad agreed that they were having fun as well. "The best part of all this, as far as I'm concerned, is the time I get to spend with all you guys. I don't worry about coming home to an argument about my being out with my son and nephews. I can come and go as I please. I even got rid of all my suits except two of them, and it's very liberating being able to shop for the kind of clothing I enjoy wearing. Hell, yesterday I stopped by a fast-food restaurant and had one of those combo meals. Never enjoyed something so much in my life. Then I had an ice cream sundae. I don't think I'd had one of those since I was just a child."

They all talked about having this or that. Going to the movies just for fun. Dad talked more about his fast-food experience. Wats was so happy they were all were getting out and about that he didn't want to go and see the women. Never again, he thought. But they'd been making their lives difficult for too long for them not to be able to just tell them to fuck off. Wats thought he might just do that, too. Tell his mom to just fuck off.

It was decided that, as a group, they'd go up there and see them in the morning. Tonight, however, was for themselves. Even Abby was going to go with them, and he was going to ask if Rayne wanted to go as well. But first, he was going to propose to her. He was going to ask the woman of his dreams if she'd spend the rest of her life with him as his wife.

Picking up flowers on his way home, he was dismayed to find a car he didn't know in the drive. Rayne hadn't said she was expecting company, so he wasn't sure who it would be. Going into the house, he stopped right inside the entrance hall when he heard shouting and screaming from Rayne and someone else. Make that two someone else's. Barkly met him in the hallway and took the flowers he'd gotten for Rayne. He asked him who was here.

"Aunts, I believe, sir. They arrived not an hour ago, and this is how they've acted. I have wanted to call the police to have them removed from here, but Rayne said she'd take care of them." He grinned. "She is doing a good job of it so far if you ask me. They seem to think she's an employee here and won't believe anything else she says to them."

"Do me a favor, Barkly. Can you go to the desk in my office and bring me the ring in the top drawer? I was going to give it to her—" Barkly hugged him. Tightly too. "I take it you're happy with the news?"

"Yes, I am, sir. Miss Rayne is a wonderful woman, and I'm glad to see you're not nearly as dumb as we've heard you are." Laughing again, he said he'd heard it from the other butlers from the larger home. "She is a good match for you. As well as someone that will not sit back on her butt when there needs to be something said. Yes, she will make a great addition to this family."

Entering the room, Barkly right behind him, Wats walked up to Rayne and pulled her into his arms for a kiss. Much, he could see, to the displeasure of the aunts. Turning to Barkly, he asked if he'd get them some refreshments, as well as something to nibble on until dinner, as he and Rayne were headed out soon.

"Now, as I'm not caught up on things going on here, why don't you two have a seat, shut up, and let my wife to be here explain to me what's going on." He looked at Rayne before speaking again. "I planned on proposing soon, but we keep getting sidetracked." The first woman—he was going to call her mustache, as she had one better than his—told him she wasn't going to shut up or have a seat. "I'm not sure where you thought I was asking you to have a seat, but I'm not going to tolerate you talking to Rayne like you are. Nor, as I said, did I ask you what was going on. Rayne, honey, why are these loud-mouthed women here?"

"They're my father's sisters. The one that is wearing pink is my Aunt Rebecca Oliver. The other, in green, is my Aunt Selma Woolen. This is my fiancé, Doctor Watson Wilkerson." Rayne huffed as she sat down on the couch. "Wats, these are the women I was telling you about when I moved in here."

She'd not said much more than that they were around, and he pretended he knew all about them. To him, they were bullies. Whatever they were there for, he wasn't going to be run over by them, nor was Rayne.

"Rayne is claiming that she is going to be living here, with you, for the rest of her life. I will decide who she lives with and for how long." Barkly brought in the tea trolley and asked Rayne if she wanted to pour. Saying that she did, he could have burst out laughing when she did just that, like a prim and proper lady. "At least you've learned a thing or two from staying here as a servant."

"I'm not his servant, as I have told you several times already. If you call me that again, Aunt Rebecca, I'm going to smash this lovely teapot upside of your head and be done with you." She smiled at the other aunt. "Would you like lemon or sugar, Aunt Selma?"

"Two, my dear. Just so you're aware, I didn't want to come here. When she saw it in the newspaper about all the students at your college being promoted to RNs, she just had to come." Wats leaned back on the couch as Rayne told her other aunt that she hadn't realized it was in the paper. "Oh my, yes. It was talking about how you and the others were taking your boards today and were going to help out with this lovely town."

"Do you mind not prattling on and on about things you do not know about?" Aunt Becky, he decided to call her, pinned him with a pointed stare. "You. What do you do for a living that makes it so you can afford this extravagant home? She said, doctor. Are you some sort of doctor that sells drugs made right here on the grounds? I wouldn't put it past my niece to do something just that way."

"What do you mean?" He turned down the cup of tea and glanced at Aunt Selma, and noticed that she was trying very hard not to laugh. Wats had had enough of women bullying him around. "I'm a doctor of medicine. My cousin, Mars, he's a chemist. He is opening a compound drug store right here in—"

She cut him off. "Why do you think I'm going to care what your cousin does, young man? I asked you what you did for a living. And I don't believe for one second that a doctor, as you're claiming to be, would attach themselves to someone like my niece. She's not what people would call refined." Wats looked at the aunts, then at Rayne. She was pissed, and he wasn't helping, he didn't think. "I demand that you call this off, whatever you call this travesty that you're pulling."

"Aunt Selma, do you think I'm lying about my love for Rayne?" She shook her head and sipped her tea. When she put it down on the table in front of her, she picked up the scone that was handed to her and nibbled on it. "Good to know."

Before he could toss the older lady out of the house, which he wanted to do badly, Mr. Oliver came into the room and looked hopping mad. The first thing he did was look at Becky and ask her what the Sam hill she was doing there.

"I've come to make sure you're being taken care of." Selma huffed this time.

"Shut your mouth, Selma. You know as well as I do that this is just a ruse to get all his money."

"What money? Last I looked in my account I had less than enough to buy me a newspaper. Rayne here would have to lend me some money before she'd be able to rob me blind. Now, tell me what you're doing here. And you'd better not be lying to me again, young lady. I'm still your father, and I'm not going to be happy with anything less than the truth. Talk." She asked him what he was doing here. "I live here. Same as Rayne does. They're getting together if my eyes are right. But this here young man has welcomed me with open arms, more than you ever did. He's been taking good care of me too. Never had anyone worry so much about me as an old man as these here two have. Got me a cell phone. Someone to cart my hiney around too. I even got me some walking around money when I need it. Now, you get your butts right back home or wherever rock you slimed your way out from under, and leave the two of us alone."

"It said in the newspaper that your home has been torn down." James looked at Selma, who shrugged, then back at Becky when she continued. "I thought it would be just like her to toss you aside and fend for herself."

"You get out of here, Becky before I have to take a switch to your backside. Don't you think I'm too old to do it either. Of all the things to say — how much have you done for me? Answer me that. Since you left home, you've not done nary a thing for either of us. Even when your momma died, you didn't bother coming around." She said she was working. "Working that evil mind you have there. I don't want you coming back here. I'm sure that Rayne and Wats here will agree with me when I tell you that if you darken the doorway here ever again, he'll call the police on you. You're a terrible person, Becky. You have an evil mind and a nasty mouth."

Becky stood up, and Wats did as well. She looked over at Selma and told her they didn't seem to be welcome here and that they were leaving. Selma picked up her scone, and Wats thought for sure she was going to ask if she could take it with her. Instead, she leaned back on the couch she was sitting in and looked at her sister.

"You're not welcome here, Becky. I am, I hope." Rayne nodded, and Selma nodded. "Thank you. I've only just decided I'd like to live close to the two of you and my dad. I think I'd enjoy having some young company around me in my golden years. Are you going to have children?"

They both answered yes that they wanted several. James danced a jig, an honest to goodness jig, right there in the living room. Then he looked at his other daughter, asking her why she was still there.

She glared at Rayne. "She's filled your head with terrible things, Father. I won't have it." Wats

stood up. "Oh, do sit down and behave before I
have to smack you around."

"Try it, and it'll be the last thing you ever do.
Now, you were told to get out of our home. You
aren't welcome here. I've had enough bullies in my
life that I don't need someone else trying to take
the wind out of my sails, as I've heard James say
several times since he's been living here. So, unless
you want to be the next headline in the newspaper
or the obits—I don't care which—you will leave
here. On your own, or I put you out." She told him
she didn't care for his tone. "Like I give a fuck what
you care for. Barkly, call the police for me, please.
Ms. Oliver has overstayed her welcome. And if you
wouldn't mind making up one of the suites for Ms.
Woolen, I do believe she's going to be staying here."

"Oh, how lovely. I'm not even going to
pretend like I don't want you to do that for me. I
believe I will enjoy this even more." Selma stood
up and kissed him on the cheek. "Yes, you're a
good man, Watson. A very good man indeed." She
looked at her niece. "Come on, Rayne, let's you and
I go find us something more substantial to have to
eat. Why don't we? I've been eating crap food long
enough. Dad, I'm so happy you've found a good
man for Rayne. She of all people deserves it."

As they left the room, he and James stood

there with Rebecca while either the police took her out or she left on her own. He wondered if she'd say she'd change her ways. But the moment she lifted her chin, he knew that there was no changing her mind about them or what was going on.

"I'm going to have you investigated. The moment I find any dirt on you, I'm going to put it in the paper." Wats didn't even bother telling her to go ahead. "You'll rue the day you messed with me, young man. See if I don't make you suffer."

"You have fun with that." The police were let into the room. "Will you show this lady off my land, Officer Donald? She's not welcome here any longer."

As she was forced out of the house, Wats turned to James. Telling him that he was sorry for what happened, the man hugged him. Telling him that he'd never been so proud of anyone in his life than him standing up to Becky.

"She's always had it in her head that her way was the only way. That's why she couldn't find herself a man. Too bossy. But I love that you did this. Wats, I'm proud to call you my grandson-in-law. You did this old man some good today." Wats said it had felt good to him as well. "Good."

After another hug, James left him in the living room. He could hear his laughter as it rang out through the house. When he got to the kitchen, Wats right behind him, the man was still laughing and having a good time. For a man in his nineties, he sure could dance like he meant to.

Chapter 5

Dinner wasn't what she'd had in mind, but Rayne was enjoying it all the same. Aunt Selma told her how she'd been wanting to leave her sister's grips for some time. Aunt Becky had moved in with her when Uncle Markus had passed away.

"I don't know what she was thinking when she did that. We've never gotten along well. And to be honest with you, I don't even know why she thought moving in with me would help me get over Markus's death. The poor old soul was so ill the last few months of his life that I think he wanted to die." She smiled at her. "Now, you'll have to tell me what I can do for you and that lovely man of yours."

"Nothing that I'm aware of. Unless you're going to be living here with Grandda and us. There is plenty of room." Aunt Selma said it was an impressive home. "I'm only just now getting used to the size of it. I love this place, and Wats."

"That is obvious on both your faces. My goodness, he certainly is in love with you." Rayne felt her face heat up. "The two of you, are you going to get married?"

They'd been in the kitchen eating a snack. As she'd been invited to have dinner with them by Wats, Grandda had decided to go as well. Wats joined them in the kitchen and took several carrots off her plate, and dipped them into the humus that had been given to them too.

"I wanted to do this later, but I think now is the perfect time." He got down on one knee and pulled out the very ornate box. "This was given to me to propose with by my Aunt Holly when she passed away. I didn't have any history with it, and it took several days for me to go to Uncle Clayton to get it."

"Can I see it?" He opened the box. "Oh, Wats, this is beautiful. But much too expensive for me to wear."

"Hush up and let him tell you the history. And just so you know, you deserve whatever this man gives you." She looked at Wats. "Go on, young man. Tell her the story about this ring. I'm betting it's a humdinger."

"It is. Very colorful, as a matter of fact. My Aunt Holly received a lot of jewelry when she was born. This was never a part of the estate, so she decided that all of us, including her son, needed something from her things for us to pass on to our own children." He looked at the ring after taking it from the box. "It belonged to my too many greats to remember them all aunt. Her name was Hester Wilkerson. She never married, but according to what Uncle Clayton knew about her, there was always someone she had on the hook. Meaning, he told me, she'd had more lovers than a woman half her age. This ring was given to her by the man that was most persistent in declaring that he loved her. Which Hester did him as well. But several days before the wedding of the decade was to be performed, Alexander Rihanoff was murdered in his own bed by one of his servants. His father, Lord Rihanoff, didn't want his son to marry an American."

"Well, that's a terrible story." He laughed and told her there was more. "I hope it's a bit cheerier than what you've said so far."

"It is. After Markus was murdered, my aunt decided to hunt down the man who had taken her love from her. Not the servant, but the man who had ordered the death. She traveled all the way to Russia — very unheard of for a woman to travel with just a maid. By the time she was in the country, her maternal state was very obvious. Another unheard of thing was a child being born out of wedlock. I'm sure it happened, but not to someone as wealthy and well known as my aunt. Anyway, the lord of the large castle wouldn't see her. But that didn't stop her from getting not only into his castle but in his bed-chamber too. She was even back then someone that men were afraid of. She was outspoken and didn't care what others thought of her, my uncle Clayton told me." He smiled at her. "The lord woke up with a blade at his throat and his balls. It's said that the man was quite taken with her mannerisms as well as her carrying a son, he hoped, of his son."

"Oh, I like this aunt of yours, Wats." Wats told Selma that he did as well. "Did she end up having the child there in Russia? Was the old bastard at least generous enough with her so that she could have fun?"

"He was indeed. He not only welcomed her and her child yet to be born into his home but also handed over the entire estate, which would have gone to his son after his marriage, to my aunt. The aunt was very pleased, but it didn't negate the fact that she'd lost the only love she would ever have. When the child was born—a girl, not a boy, as he so hoped—my aunt decided she couldn't bring a child home with her without causing trouble for the rest of her family. Leaving the little girl there was, according to the story, one of the hardest things she'd ever done. But it was meant to be because when the older Rihanoff passed away, he left her everything as his only living relative." Rayne asked him what happened after that. "Well, the story goes that the child grew up to be a beautiful, headstrong woman. She doubled the estate and gave her husband six children — five boys, then a little girl was born last. Her husband was her exact opposite in all things except for his love for his pretty bride. When the time came for her sons to take over the lands and castle, she and her husband and her two youngest sons moved to America. The daughter wanted to stay in her home country because, like her mother, she was marrying for love, not for need of more lands."

"She married a Wilkerson. This child of your aunt, she bore the first Wilkerson and brought them here to find their own loves." Wats smiled as he nodded. "Oh, I love this story. I'm going to tell it to our children. It did have a nice happy ending, and I love you for telling it to me. Oh, Wats, I love you with all my heart."

"And I love you." He slipped the ring on her finger, then kissed her palm. "If you'd not mind,

I'd like to arrange for us to be married as soon as possible. Then again, if you don't mind, I'd like to start a family with you. Have lots of children that grow up to be just like their mother."

"I don't know about all that." Aunt Selma laughed and stood up. Rayne asked her if she was leaving. "No. I need to get my things from the hotel. I'm ever so grateful that I had a separate room from Becky. She would have tossed them out if I hadn't. Also, I have a few things I need to look into. Are you sure you don't mind me staying here for a few days? Just to get myself a little home I can care for?"

"I'll talk to Mars. He has a lot of condos and rentals. Perhaps he might have one open that you can take." Rayne liked that idea. She'd be close, but not too close. Laughing, she hugged her aunt when she said she'd love to see her more often now that she was going to be close. "My dad and uncles live there, as well as Mars until his house is finished. He and Abby have had the entire place redone."

"You're very wealthy, aren't you, young man?" Wats said he was comfortable. It was Mars that was very wealthy. "I like you, Wats. Very much. I don't think if I had been looking the world over, I could have found a better person for Rayne than you. She's a very lucky woman."

"Thank you. It's me that is lucky. To have

found someone as wonderful and loving as Rayne makes me the luckiest person in the world." After hugging them both, Aunt Selma left them to go pick up her things. "Looks like we have the house to ourselves."

Shaking her head, she told him about dinner plans that they were enjoying right now. "I thought — well, honestly, I love that idea. To have dinner with the two people in the world that seem to have nothing to gain or want from us. It's refreshing." She told him he was a sap. "You might not think so when I take you to see the mothers tomorrow. There are only three of them left, but they make you think there are three times that many."

Getting home late, Rayne fell into bed and was asleep before she thought the light was off. It had been a stressful day, and tomorrow wasn't going to be any better. She was glad that she'd spoken to Abby and Amy about the women. Rayne decided she'd not let them bully her around as she was told they'd do.

Waking up to a scream spilling from her mouth, she looked down at Wats as he grinned at her. His face was wet with her cream, his smile telling her that he wasn't nearly done with her. She asked him what the hell he was doing.

"I must be doing something wrong if you need

to ask me. I'll just double up my efforts this time around." She squeezed her legs together, and that had him laughing. "You're sending mixed signals, love. Do you want me to keep drinking from you, or are you finished with me? I want you to be happy."

"If I were any happier right now, they'd lock me up. What I meant to ask you was, is this going to be the norm? I mean, the way you wake me up? Because if it is, I'm afraid that I won't survive my days." He kissed her thigh as he watched her. "You look satisfied right now. You're not, are you?"

Instead of answering her, he sat up between her legs. His cock was dark with blood, and dripping from the tip was the most delicious thing she'd ever seen. Reaching down after sitting up in the bed, she touched the tip and took his creaminess to her mouth. Her moan found her on her back and Wats kissing her.

He touched her everywhere while he worked her mouth over — her breasts, ear lobes, as well as her shoulders and ribs. Wats would touch her someplace, and she'd think that was the most erotic place on her body. Then he'd move, and she'd realize he'd found another place that she thought was too much for her.

Wats had his cock at her clit. Each time he moved, even if it was just to adjust himself to another position, she'd feel it touching off some part of her. Never would Rayne have thought a woman's clit was connected to every nerve ending in her entire body.

"I want you to come for me. When you do, I'm going to take you." She knew what he was telling her, and it made her tense up, knowing it was going to be painful. "If you tense up on me now, Rayne, we're never going to leave this bedroom."

"Why?" He told her. "Oh. Yes, I can see where people would notice that you're hard as stone and your balls are blue. Why are they called that? Blue balls, I mean?"

She didn't get an answer. Or perhaps she did, and she didn't hear it over her own screaming release. She felt his cock enter her, stretching her open and filling her to her throat. There wasn't much in the way of pain, but the pleasure of it was too much, and she simply checked out for a few seconds. When she woke, Wats was saying her name softly, but Rayne had an idea that he was starting to panic just a little.

"I love you." He moved, his cock no longer painful being inside of her, but causing deep, whole body pleasure. Moving with him to his push, she pushed back. Rayne was feeling a climax coming up and over her that she knew was going to take her to a place yet undiscovered by anyone else. "Watson, I love you."

It took her. For several seconds, she couldn't breathe. Couldn't hear. It was as if her entire system had shut down to get as much enjoyment out of their coming together as it could. When she took in a deep breath, with the second tidal wave of pleasure, stronger than the first, she felt her eyes flicker closed. If not for Wats, holding her to his body when he joined her in the third climax, she was sure she would have died right then and there with a big smile on her face and her body a puddle of relaxed muscle and skin.

Rayne woke up quickly. Sitting up in the bed, she looked around. Alone in the big bed, she cocked her head when she heard something. It was Wats. He was singing in the shower, some old tune her grandda sang when he thought no one was about in the house.

Getting up, she pulled on his shirt that had been dropped on the floor and went into the bathroom where he was. Just as he was stepping out of the stall, she handed him a warmed towel. Wats kissed her and asked her if she was going with him.

"I am. I feel like I can take on the world right now." He told her to hurry, but not too much. They had about an hour. "I am a little sore, to be honest with you. But it's a good kind of sore. Don't you think?"

"I think you nearly killed me." She wrapped her arms around his shoulders as he held her. "I have never, not since I learned about sex, enjoyed something so profoundly as I did this morning. If we do that very often, I'm sure I'll be an old, yet happy man in a comatose state."

She was still laughing when she stepped into the shower stall and had hot water hit her body. Christ, she was sore everywhere. Smiling, she tenderly washed up, thinking he was right. If they had sex like this every day, she'd be dead as well.

~*~

Wats and Rayne rode up to the prison with his dad. Dad had mentioned that he wanted to take them out to dinner after this was finished, and it made more sense for them to ride together. It wasn't going to be a good thing, what they were doing today, but it would be over. The aunts having been found guilty of murder, as well as a long list of other crimes, ones he never knew about. Wats wasn't looking forward to seeing his mom, nor hearing her drivel about how she'd done nothing wrong and they should get her out. It wasn't going to happen.

The prison was ready for them when they

arrived. Abby had worn a blood-red dress, much like the one his mother had worn to Aunt Holly's funeral. When he looked at the other two, he could see they'd taken their cues from Abby and wore similar dresses. He thought it was the funniest thing he could have seen. He loved the three of them to pieces for doing this.

Wats was sure that Mars didn't want to be there. He had to know that they were going to take potshots at him about his being a bastard son. How he wasn't worth the time of day, and how everything bad that had happened in their lives would be put squarely on his shoulders. However, looking at him right now, he thought Mars wasn't going to take it any more than the others were. He wanted to see them all, Mars and his uncles, get the kind of freedom they deserved.

His mother was the first person in the room. Of course, nothing was to her liking, and she tried very hard to get someone to take the chains off her wrists and ankles. The guards didn't even blink when she started jerking the chains from them and cursing. Wats couldn't help it. He laughed.

"What the fuck do you think is so funny? Finding your mother chained up like a dog? Watson, get your ass over here and make them release me." He asked her if she wanted to hug him. "If that will get your ass in gear, then sure, why the fuck not? I know you studied law. Make them let me go."

"I'm a doctor, not an attorney. Even if I was one, I'd gladly pay them to keep you hogtied where you are." She cursed at him again. "You don't know shit about me, do you, Tina?"

"You're to give me the respect that I deserve, or so help me, I'm going to teach you a few lessons when I get out of here. And I will, by God, even if your father needs to sell off everything we own for me to get out." Dad laughed, and so did Rayne. "Laugh it up, bitch. I don't know what part you're playing in this little circus going on around here, but you'll regret having any kind of relationship with my husband. Not that I want him, but if I can't have him, no one can. Do you hear that, Wesley? I'm going to— What are you wearing? Are those blue jeans? Christ, I'm going to have to start from scratch with you, aren't I? You don't get too comfortable in those nasty things, Wesley Wilkerson. As soon as I'm free, I'm going to—"

"Oh, will you shut the fuck up? Christ love a duck, you do go on, don't you?" Mother looked at Rayne and told her to keep her slutty mouth shut. "My slutty mouth? Honey, no one has anything on your mouth. I heard that you've sucked off every male within a ten-mile radius of the little town we live in. And I'm not a slut, you fucking moron. I'm Wat's wife. I'm so glad I never got to meet you before all this went down. Or maybe I would have just taken you out and been done with you."

"You aren't my son's anything, you cunt. I'll say when he can marry and to whom. And when he marries, it will be someone like me." Rayne laughed, and he and his dad leaned back and let Rayne take over. "What the hell is so funny now?"

"You and the other women. Thinking that you're going to get out. You're not. Not unless it's in a black body bag and you're no longer breathing." Mother said she lied. "No. Again, that would be you. Because of your stupidity in deciding that you all should have the same trial, did you know that you've been charged with the murder of Eita Wilkerson, as well as Holly Wilkerson? Yeah, when you lumped all the stupid people into one trial, you get them all. Here, let me read it to you."

"I did nothing to murder our dear Eita. Sure, I had a hand in a couple of the things around town, but I had nothing to do with Eita being dead." Rayne picked up the paperwork from the attorney's office. "Give that to me. You have no rights to anything with my name on it. You probably can't read anyway. I heard that your kind is as stupid as they come."

"I can read this just fine." The other two women came into the room then and were chained to their places too. But they were far apart, Wats noticed. He wondered if that was by plan or necessity. "Fourteen counts of murder in the first degree. Twelve counts of murder in the second degree. Intent to do harm to a federal officer. Murder of a federal sitting judge. You guys sure do like to kill off people, don't you? Robbery. Manslaughter. Prostitution. Selling of a minor. Well, I'm sure you guys know the rest of this list. I mean, they did tell you this, like fifty times when you got here. By the way, do you have memory issues? That's the only reason I can think of that you'd be thinking you've done nothing wrong. I mean, seriously, there isn't any way you can think you're getting out of here unless you have some sort of dementia or have had a stroke." Rayne turned to him. "Did your mother dearest have a stroke, Wats?"

"His name is Watson, and no, I have not had a stroke. I can remember things very well, and you can bet that I'm going to get you when I—"

"Yes, yes, I know. When you get out of here. You're not, so I'm not worried about you any more than I am the other two women you're locked up with. You're just lucky that Ohio is no longer using lethal injection to kill off dirtbags like you."

Rayne got close to his mother, and he stood up. If she so much as harmed Rayne, he'd kill his mother without a second thought. They all watched as Mother leapt at Rayne, gnashing her teeth at her like a wild animal. "Yes, it really is too bad. I mean, if they would allow it, I'd take you out right now so that no one has to fuck with you and the other two. I just had a thought. You went from being the bitches five to only three of you. To me, that's good. Perhaps you guys will continue to kill each other off or yourself, and the state will save a good deal of money."

"I loathe you." Rayne smiled at his mother. "When I get out of here—"

Rayne slapped his mother hard enough to jerk her head around. Blood poured from a split on her lip, and her cheek bore the print of her hand. When Mother started to speak again, Rayne hit her twice more.

No one moved in the room, not the guards nor any of the family that had come up here. Mother seemed as shocked as he'd ever seen her. It wasn't until his dad started applauding that Wats knew this was about the best way to deal with someone like his mother.

"You've been told quite enough that you're not getting out of here. None of you are. If I have to stand here and slap you around until you understand, I will. Say it after me, Tina, I'm not getting out of here." Mother said she was and that she was going to kill her — another slap to her face, more blood on her nose and lips now. "You're not going to get any help from anyone in this room, Tina. I'd learn quicker if I were you."

"I'm going to — " This time, Rayne hit her with her doubled-up fist. Not only did his mother's head snap back, but blood splattered down the front of her and Penny behind her. "Hit me again and — "

So Rayne hit her again. "I can do this all day. And I'm sure if I get a little tired, Abby or Amy will take over for me. Won't you, ladies?" They both stood up. Abby pulled off her sweater and started shadow punching like she was getting ready to have her turn. "See? We've all learned that you're not going to get out of prison. As soon as you learn it, we'll be on our way. And you should also understand this. None of us will return. Not for any of the three of you. There will be no funeral for the three of you. I'm going to talk Wats into donating your body to science. I'm sure they can find out what the fuck made you such a terrible person. Or not. I don't know. But you can bet that no one will make a fuss about your deaths, nor will they…well, they might well have a celebration. We might even have the town's mayor make it a holiday. No kiddies in school that day. The mail will be paused. Yes, I can see that happening. What do you think, Clayton? You can do that when you're mayor, right?"

"You're nothing but a cheap piece of ass." Rayne laughed and told her now that she was Wat's wife, she didn't have to be cheap. They had all kinds of money. "Watson, you're to get this piece of trash out of my sight. I have had enough of your little fun with me."

"No. And if you call her trash or slut once more, I'm going to take over where Rayne left off and beat you until you scare small children when they see you. If you were to ever be able to see small children." Wats stood up, and the rest of them did as well. "I'd like to say this has been fun—some of it has been—but it certainly gives us all a sense of freedom. You're dead to me, Tina. I have no mother. As far as I'm concerned, Holly was my mother, and you—you're nothing. We, none of us, will return. You are, as of the moment we leave here, on your own. The warden is going to treat you like any other inmate behind bars. No more pacifying your sense of entitlement. Good luck with your life. Or not. I don't give a shit what happens to you from now on."

They left then. He and Rayne were the only

two left behind when first his uncles walked out the door, then his cousins. Wats turned to his mother once more before he and Rayne left as well.

"I hate you. I thought you should know that before I'm out of here. I hate you with a passion that I will never have for another being. You took the life of the greatest person I've ever known. You even took years from my being with my father that I won't ever forgive you for. My children will never know you. None of us will name our children for any of you. As far as we're all concerned, you died the moment you took the life of Holly." He walked out the door holding Rayne's hand.

His mother and the other two were screaming at them to come back. The more steps he took away from the room they'd been in, the more stress was lifted from his shoulders. By the time he was in his dad's car, getting a hug from him, Wats knew that he was going to be all right. They survived their mother. A great many people couldn't say that, sadly.

"I nearly wet myself when you hauled off and knocked his mother back off her butt, honey." Dad was still laughing when he hugged Rayne, who was nursing her bruised knuckles. "I tell you, Rayne, you're the best thing that has happened to me in a good long time. I hope you never change. Never."

"What if our children are like me? What will you say then?" Dad looked at him, then back at Rayne. "We do want a lot of kids, Wesley. I hope you don't mind that."

"I will never be happier than when a baby of my son is put into my arms to hold for the first time. And Rayne, if any of them are like you, that will just be butter on my toast." Dad got into the car. He was blowing his nose, so Wats held Rayne to give him a minute.

"I think you touched something in my dad that no one has ever touched before." Rayne laid her head on his chest. "I love you, my heart. How about we make it official and get hitched up tomorrow if I can arrange it? I have to tell you, however, I'm worried about marrying a slut."

She smacked him on the arm and got into the car. Wats was laughing when he turned back to the prison and looked at the high wire, then the armed guards in the turrets. There were people in the yard, all of them with the same uniform on, a drab gray with nothing much to distinguish one from the other.

This was the perfect place for his mother and aunts. He wished they'd been there before they'd killed his Aunt Holly, but he also knew things had to go the way they did in order for them to have what they had now. The timeline of life, Abby called it, was something they had to think of rather than what they'd lost. Without the events that were in place, he would never have gotten closer to his dad. Never have met Rayne. Things, he knew, he'd cherish forever.

Chapter 6

Tina didn't know what to think right now. Her mouth was sore and was going to need stitches, they told her. One of the officers told her she'd likely get both her eyes blackened. That didn't sit well with her, so she asked for someone to go to her house and get her makeup. Of course, no one moved to do as she bid them.

When she asked why no one had come to her aid when she'd been abused, all of them, even people that weren't in the room, said they'd seen nothing. That she'd fallen. Well, she was going to get to the bottom of this. Heads were going to roll, by God.

"All right, inmate. You sit right there, and we'll fix you right up." Tina never, when she had a choice, did what someone told her to do the first time.

It was a source of pride for her to be argumentative whenever possible. Eita would have been so proud of— "We do this the easy way, which is you sitting in this chair, or I knock you out and stitch you up while you're under. It's no sweat off my back."

"Your bedside manner is wonderful. I'm betting that is why you're here putting stitches in people that have been abused." She told her she was like her. "Doubtful. I'm a Wilkerson. I am well above anyone here. Most of the world, too, I would imagine."

"I'm an inmate like you, dumbass. I killed my husband." Tina jerked back from the woman so quickly that they both went to the floor. "What is it with you, bitch? You want someone to hurt you? Sit the fuck still, or so help me—"

"I'm not going to allow an inmate to touch me." The woman was larger than Tina by a great deal, but it was a matter of principle now. No criminal was going to touch her. "Get a real doctor here right this minute. I'll not allow— My son. He said he was some sort of doctor. Call him back in here to do this for me. It's the least he can do since I'm not at home yet."

"You're not going to be going home either. You're here for three lifetimes. You were told that several times. Also, you were told that no one from your family will come back here." The woman laughed. "At least my family will come to see me. Every weekend, like clockwork."

"They'll have to come and get me." At least Tina hoped so. A pinch to her arm was all the warning she got before she simply fell back on the floor. "Fucking bitch."

When she woke up, she was tied to a bed by leather straps. Trying to lift her head made her sick, so she just closed her eyes and laid there. After what felt like forever, she started calling for someone to come and get her. Tina wasn't used to being treated this way, damn it. She wanted to go home and be pampered.

"There you are. How do you feel?" She told the criminal that she was sick to her belly. "Yes, I guess you might be. But it's done now, and as soon as a guard comes to get you, you can go to your new room."

"I have a new room? Oh, how wonderful." She was so excited she nearly forgot about being chained up. "I do hope my family sent me some of my things. I think when I leave here, I'll just leave them behind. Surely he wouldn't have brought up my good things for this place."

"Good things? You don't have anything. You don't pay attention well, do you? You're getting a new place to live, not a new makeover. Speaking of which, you should have a look at my handiwork. Your lip is going to be scarred, I'm afraid, but nothing I can do about that." She told her she'd be able to get her face done when she got home. "Yeah, you keep thinking that, and they'll put you in a locked cell for your time here."

When the guard came to get her, Tina was giddy with excitement. Of course, the man didn't say a word to her, not answering any of her questions. Before they entered a set of doors she'd never seen before, he finally turned to her.

"You are no longer to get special treatment around here." She asked him if he thought she was getting any in the first place. "You have been. All three of you have been. However, the moment your ex-husband told us that he wasn't going to have anything to do with you, we figured he'd be all right with you being put in the general population. You and the other two will be with all the other inmates."

"I don't understand." He nodded as if he'd expected her to say that, and the door was opened that they were by. Peeking in, she saw that there were three other people in the room she was standing by. "Where is my room? I mean, I haven't had to share with anyone before this. I don't want to now. Do you know that they're criminals? I'm not."

"You are as well, Inmate. You're just like all the other women in here. A criminal. However, these two ladies will be leaving here in a few weeks. We thought we'd introduce you to prison life easily." She started to back away from the room. "Don't make this hard, Inmate. This is where you're going to be spending the rest of your life. This will be your cell."

"No. I don't want to be in there. My family — " He said no one was coming to get her. "They will. They're just upset with me because we killed that bitch Holly. But I'm a Wilkerson, and we have to keep the bloodline pure. She wasn't anything but a slut."

"You're no longer anything but Inmate. If you have to be referred to, your number on your shirt there is what you'll be going by. Remember that number. I've already been told that you'll not get any mail from anyone. There isn't a fund set up for you, so you'll need to work for — "

"I've never worked a day in my life, and I have no intentions of doing so now. You'll just have to bill my husband for this." He shook his head and said that wasn't how things were done. "Well, perhaps you should change your rules for special people like me."

"Look, Ruth, she thinks she's special." The two women in the cell laughed. "Nobody is special around here, girl. You're just going to have to get friendly with a couple of dykes, and you'll be fine. Just make sure you get you a nice big girlfriend, or you'll be beating them off. Get it? Beating them off."

She didn't get it. When Tina was shoved into the room, she fell over her chains. When told to come to the door, she thought for sure she was being played with, that they had no intentions of keeping her locked up like this. When the door slammed shut, the guard told her to put her hands in the opening, and he'd unchain her.

"This isn't right. Someone is playing a joke on me." The sound of the slamming door was still ringing in her ears as she put her hands into the opening. "I don't think this is funny at all. You're to let me out of here, or so help me I'm going to own your ass."

His gun was right there. She only had to wait for one second when she was freed, then she'd show him what a Wilkerson did when things didn't go their way. Tina didn't count on the snappy thing being on it, but she was able to wrestle it out without much in the way of trouble.

"Back up." He lifted his hands up but didn't move. "You heard me, move back, or I move you back."

The two behind her were plastered against the wall. They weren't saying a word of encouragement to her, so she ignored them. As soon as the guard told her she was going to get herself killed, she waved the gun in the direction of his head and fired.

She'd not counted on him moving too. Oh well, Tina thought, one less thing she'd have to worry about. Yelling for Penelope and Salma, she went to get them out of their cells. They were getting out of there, or she'd have to roll a few more heads.

"I don't have a key. Can you get out?" Penelope was closest to her, so she fired another shot at the lock. The scream had her looking at the criminals in Penelope's cell, and she realized she'd hit her best friend. "I didn't mean to kill you, Penelope. I'm so sorry. But I don't have a key."

Not even bothering with Salma, she made her way down the stairs. There were a lot of guards there, and all of them had their guns pointed in her direction. They'd not hurt her. She knew this because she was a Wilkerson.

"I'm going to go home and get some of my things. I'll come back if I can." No one moved, but they did tell her to put the gun down. "If I do that, you're not going to let me go home. I just need a few hours to go there. Perhaps a couple of days now that I think about it. Then I'll come back."

She smiled at them and felt her lip split open again. That had to be taken care of too. She was going to have to go under the knife. Telling them what she was going to have to do about her mouth, they told her once again to put the gun down.

"My husband used to be an attorney. He'll sue your asses if you hurt me. Just call me a cab and let me go home. You'll see. Once I'm fixed up, I'll come back. But I won't be treated like a criminal." The first sharp pain took her breath away. Looking down at herself, she saw that her shirt now had a hole in it. "You shot me? Why? I'm cooperating."

The second time a gun fired, she fell to her knees. This wasn't the way to treat her. She was the oldest living Wilkerson wife. There should have been respect given to her, not gunshots into her shirt.

It was then that she heard a volley of guns going off. Nothing could have prepared her for the pain now. She fell to her back and knew that somehow it was going to take her longer to get this taken care of. Firing her own gun, lifting her arm up to do so, Tina saw her wrist shatter, her arm covered in blood, the gun disappearing bringing on so much pain that she screamed. There was something leaking into her eyes. Not having the strength to keep her bloodied arm up any longer, she let it fall to her side. Opening her eyes when she heard her name, Tina looked up at the man dressed all in white.

"Jesus?" He said he was a doctor. "That other woman said that to me too. But she was a criminal. I want to go home."

"I'm afraid it's much too late for that, Inmate." It was getting harder and harder for her to concentrate on things. Even her breathing was hard to make work. "There is no one to notify of her death, I'm assuming?"

When the person she couldn't see said there was no one, Tina wondered who they were talking about. It must have been Penelope, she thought. It had been an accident, killing her. Surely no one would hold that against her. Penelope was her friend, not a criminal like the rest of these monsters. Tina just wanted to go home. Take a bath. Dress up nicely. Closing her eyes, she knew she'd overcome this. Knew too that she'd be going home as soon as someone fixed her up.

~*~

Wats was sitting on the deck when his dad joined him. Late last night, a guard from the prison, someone he'd gone to school with, had called him directly. His mother was dead, as was Penelope.

Then this morning, he'd gotten a second call from him. Salma had killed herself like Christa had, chewing out her wrists and bleeding out. He hadn't any idea if his dad knew or even wanted to know, so he told him about the baby he delivered last night.

"She's so beautiful, Dad. And perfect. To me anyway. A head full of the reddest hair I've ever seen. Weighed in at nine pounds fourteen ounces." Dad asked him if the mother was all right too. "The mother, only sixteen, left today without her. She knows, she told the head nurse, that she couldn't care for her the way she'd need to be. Plus, her parents would only allow her to come home if she didn't have the child with her."

"Why do you suppose parents do that to their kids? I guess I can understand that a little. If the child is promiscuous, I guess. I'm not even sure that is a good enough reason. But they'd just put her in a spot that will change the course of her life and that of her parents." He wondered if his dad was thinking of his own sister and confirmed that when he spoke again. "Holly needed us, and even though she was only a mile away, not one of us went to check on her. See if she was doing all right. I feel the worst about that, I think. Your mother is dead."

"I know. All three of them are." Dad nodded. "I'm thinking of adopting the infant. I've spoken to

Rayne about it, and she's going there now to see her."

Dad looked at him so quickly that he thought something had happened. "Are you serious? I mean, yes, you are. You're forever serious about things. I have learned a great deal about you in the— Are you going to make me a grandfather, Wats?"

"I have to wait on Rayne to approve. I don't know why she'd not, but then, we're just getting to know each other a little more each day. We have had plans to be married the last few days, but something is forever coming up." He looked at his dad and saw that he was crying. "Don't do that, Dad. If you start sobbing, we're both going to be a mess when Rayne comes home, and that won't be good. She'll make fun of us."

"She will at that." Dad laughed, then looked out over the yard. "You'll need to put in a fence in place for her when she's able to play in the yard. I just realized that I don't know a great deal about babies and children."

"I only know them when they're first born. After that, I'm a little lost. But I'm sure we'll all do fine." He heard someone in the house but didn't say anything to his dad. They were having a nice talk, and he didn't want anyone to ruin it for them. "My practice is up and running again. I told you about

Rayne going to the hospital to work. She's expecting to hear from the boards any day now. They're sort of rushing it through so the nurses that took the test will be able to start working right away."

"I know she'll do well on the test. She's one smart woman." Dad laughed a little—it sounded sort of forced and sad. "I can still see her smacking around Tina. Best feeling I ever had concerning her. I know it's not nice, but it is what it is, I suppose. I cannot wait to see you with a child in your arms. Any of you, for that matter. It'll be like everything prior to that day will be erased away, and we're starting anew. Does that make sense?"

He never got a chance to answer his dad. Rayne came out of the house with a bundle in her arms. When she started to come around and hand the baby over to him, he nodded toward his father. Nodding once, Rayne put their newest family member into his dad's arms.

"Wesley, this is our daughter, Allison Jane Wilkerson. We're thinking of calling her AJ for short." Dad started sobbing when Rayne pulled the little blanket off the baby's face. "We were hoping you'd be here when we got home today. She's all ours right now."

The baby stared at his dad like she was studying him. When she yawned, Dad pulled her closer to his body, holding her like she was the most precious thing he'd ever touched. Then he looked at him.

"You knew." He said he had. "You knew you were going to be bringing her home. Son, you have no idea how much I needed this right now."

"I think we all needed something fresh to come out of this." Rayne looked at him while she finished. "I don't have a great deal of experience with children, but I figure we can learn as we go. From what I've been told, you usually mess up your first one anyway."

"Yes, I've heard that as well. But it's doubtful to anyone who knows you two that you would ever allow that to happen. She sure is a beautiful little thing, isn't she?" Dad pulled away the blanket and looked at AJ's hands and toes. "Perfect, just like you said. Look at those chubby little legs. I'm betting she'll be chasing butterflies in no time."

They went into the house when the baby started fussing. The weather was just a little too cool for her, he supposed. Lighting the fireplace, Dad sat on the floor and took the baby's shirt off. That was all she had on besides her diaper. Dad counted her toes, tickled her little feet, and kissed every part of her. Rayne sat down by him while the two of them watched his dad with their daughter.

"My aunt and Grandda are going to be jealous now. Not that I care. They'll get to know her soon enough. Tell me what you think of the staff there asking if we'd be willing to be foster parents of newborns when they come in. All I can think of is we'll have a houseful of Wilkerson children if we do that." He laughed and told her that's what happened with AJ. "I bet. All they had to do was put her in my arms, and I knew I'd be bringing her home. Something so warm and fuzzy about holding a baby. Don't you think?"

"She's going to be very popular with her new great uncles too, I'm thinking. Also, we can't tell them any mistakes we make. If we do, they'll learn from them and be better at this than we will."

"We can't have that." He laughed with her. "We do need to get her some things to wear. The staff made sure I knew the things we'd need, as well as the things parents fall for and don't need. That list is longer than the one that she needs."

"I did know that. When I'm delivering a baby, that's what all the parents are told by the staff. Only buy what you need for a week. Nothing will be as useful as the stores make them out to be. You have no idea how many times I've had mothers come back for their check-up to tell me that the nurses were right." Rayne handed him the list of things they needed to get. "I can go into town and get the essentials if you'd like to stay here with AJ and Dad."

"She'll need a few sleepers too, I was told. Really, it's all she needs to wear around to keep her warm." Rayne looked at him with such sadness on her face. "I wanted to pick out some cute little outfits for her too."

As much as they didn't want to leave AJ at home, Dad said he'd make sure he never left her. It was Rayne that told him that she'd be all right with him. Dad looked like she'd given him the keys to the castle just then. Leaving her behind, however, was about as hard as it could get, he thought.

They were still deciding on the sleepers when he just took them away from Rayne and put them in the cart. It wasn't as if they couldn't afford anything the baby needed and didn't need, he told her. After that, she started picking out cute girly outfits, but only two. She would grow out of them quickly if they got her any more than that.

Formula was something they'd had to call Dad about. Neither of them could remember what kind they'd been given at the hospital. Dad whispered his answers to them as AJ had fallen asleep on his lap. Then they'd had to call him a second time when they were in the diaper section. Dad seemed to be having the time of his life with AJ and helping them out as well.

They were home later than they'd thought they'd be. Dad was still on the floor with AJ, but he did tell them that he'd been up and around too. Dad told them that he'd fed her, one of the best things he'd ever experienced. Then he said he was sorry.

"For what? Feeding your granddaughter when she was hungry?" Dad told him why he was sorry. "Dad, don't think of that. Don't worry that you didn't feed me bottles when I was a baby. That's all in the past. AJ is giving you an opportunity to make up for things that you missed because of Mother. Our daughter will absolutely love you being there for her because I have no doubt that you're going to be her hero in all things."

"I've never been a hero to anyone." Wats told his dad that he was his hero now. "I don't believe you have any doubt that I was a screw-up. That I messed up royally with not just you, but I think I let a great many people down."

"Are you still doing that?" He said he'd not planned on it. "So, as I said, it's over and done with. They're gone. Not just out of our lives, Dad. But gone to the point where we don't need to worry about them or their deeds from now on. You've said that you feel like a new man. Then be one. I need you to just move on as though you've been given a new life. A fresh slate, if you wish."

Dad looked down at AJ—watching her sleep was the most relaxing thing he'd witnessed. When Dad started talking, he didn't know at first if he was explaining things to him or his daughter. Either way, he could almost hurt for his dad.

"I need to tell you this one thing, then I'm going to take your advice and not think of any of them ever again. When we first heard that Holly was going to have a baby, I went to see her. I was there for about twenty minutes when Tina found out where I was and came after me. As I said, I wasn't there long, but I did get to see that she was doing all right. I gave her ten thousand dollars. I don't know why, but it felt like I needed to do something. Then Tina showed up." Dad looked at him while he continued. "She beat Holly. Beat her so severely that she was bleeding badly. Me too, but I wasn't going to have a child, and I was terrified for my sister. Calling the police, the only thing I could think to do, they came just as the other four of them showed up."

"Christ." Dad nodded. He put his finger into AJ's hand, and she curled her fingers around it. "Dad, you don't have to finish the story."

"But I do, Wats. I really need to finish this."

Nodding, he watched his dad as tears rolled down his cheeks. "It was a nightmare. Holly was taken to the hospital while the others stayed behind to teach me a lesson. And what a lesson it was. I had three broken ribs on my right, two on the left. My wrist was shattered, and my jaw had been broken. I had to eat liquids for three months. And your mother managed to be home when I was ready to eat. She would heat my food up so hot that it burned me. And she was right there making sure that I drank every drop of it before I could be finished."

Sobbing now, Dad finished the story. He told him how he'd never gone against them again, not in all these years. That occasionally he'd be cornered by any one of them, and they'd remind him again, harshly.

"Then one day, after Tina had left, Holly came by. She wouldn't come into the house. Didn't want to sit on the back deck either. She just wanted to make sure I was all right. That nothing too bad had happened to me." Dad cried harder. "I was so worried that Tina would find her there. Don't you see what a coward I was? Instead of making sure my sixteen year old sister was all right, I was worried that I'd get caught by my wife and her friends."

There were no words for him to give to his dad to comfort him. Wats had felt the wrath of his mother and her friends. It hadn't stopped him from seeing Holly, but he had friends. There were the other cousins there to help him. Not that it was a good reason for his dad to have gone for his own comfort over his child sister. But Wats also knew to hold this against his father wasn't going to make either of their lives any better.

So, instead of telling his father he was a coward—Wats never thought that—or that he was ashamed of him—which he wasn't—he did the only thing that would heal them both. He pulled his father up from the floor and hugged him as tightly as he could.

Dad held onto him as if he was never going to let go. Wats thought it might be the thing they both needed, to hold onto each other like it meant their very lives. Because in a lot of ways, it did. When Dad seemed to calm down, he sat on the couch after picking up AJ.

"Do you know why I think you're going to be good at being a father? Because you're braver than I am. Smarter too." He started to tell his dad that it wasn't true when he handed him AJ. "I have to take a walk for a little while. I'll be back in time for dinner. I need this. Just a few minutes to me. All right?"

"Yes. So long as you know to come back

here." Wats knew what he was telling his dad, not
to do something stupid. It took his dad a little longer
than he thought it should have for him to answer.
However, he said he'd be back. He promised. When
he left, Wats looked at his daughter. "You're going
to have to keep an eye on Grandpa, little one. He
needs you more than we do, I think."

After a while, he and AJ took a nap on the
sofa. The room was nice and warm, her diaper was
dry, and she had on the cutest little sleeper that
Rayne had picked out. He still had to tell the rest of
his family that he was a father.

Sitting up, Wats nearly spilled AJ to the floor.
"Holy Christ, honey, I'm a father."

He didn't tell Rayne his revelation. He was
sure she'd call him a dork or something like that. So
when she came into the room with them, he shared
the couch with her and didn't say a word. Sometimes
things were better left untold. Wats knew he'd be
teased less if he kept that little part to himself.

Chapter 7

Rayne didn't want to go to work today. She had gotten the shift she wanted and more money than she'd thought she'd be making at this point in her career, but she wanted to be home with AJ and watching her grow. Rayne was sure AJ was growing every thirty seconds, and if she wasn't there during that time, she'd miss something important.

"Nurse Wilkerson? Mr. Elliot wants you to come to his office. He said to tell you that you're not in trouble, but he would like to speak to you." Nodding, she left the floor she was on to head to his office. She was glad for the break, actually. They'd been busy all day.

The football season had started up three days ago. Seven injuries were game-related, and she had to laugh every time she thought of the parents being hurt and not the kids. Apparently, when you used your screaming voice at a close game for nearly four hours, things were painful to swallow.

She knocked on the door before going in. Mr. Elliot was sitting there with not just the head of nursing but Wats as well.

"Everything is all right, honey." She didn't care. Kissing him on the mouth, she took AJ from him and held her. It was that or hurt someone to make them tell her what the hell was going on. "You've gotten your test scores back. Mr. Elliot wouldn't tell us until you arrived. That's all."

"I failed, didn't I? I knew I should have waited to take my exams. Now I'll have to—" She looked at Wats, then at Mr. Elliot. "I'm sorry, what did you say?"

"You had the wrong test given to you. I don't know why you'd be aware of that, but you just took the test like you should have without questioning anything." Mr. Elliot laughed hard. "I've never in all my life been so happy to tell someone that. You took the wrong test, and not only did you pass it with flying colors, but you aced it. You got every single question correct. Even the ones that most people get wrong. Congratulations, honey."

"I don't understand." She was handed her paperwork. But only giving it a little glance, she handed it to Wats. "Shouldn't you be upset? I mean, this means I can't work in the hospital until I take the correct one, right?"

"Usually, but the board had a special meeting concerning you and your test score. They decided, after a few hours of research and deliberation, that your score stands as is." She looked at Wats when he laughed. "You took the state boards for being a medical doctor, Rayne. You passed a test that should have tripped you up. But not only did you sail over that, but you also didn't get a single question wrong. You're going to be adding M.D. to your name from now on."

He handed her a gift, and she opened it up. The paper was beautiful in that it had stethoscopes all over it with a pretty yellow bow. Inside it was a lab coat with her name on it. Dr. R. Wilkerson, M.D. She touched the letters there and looked at Wats.

"This is yours, isn't it?' He shook his head and told her it was hers, and rightfully so. "I really did pass the boards for being a doctor? And they're going to let me be one?"

"Yes. There was only one other person that did that well. She missed one. I believe you know her too. Charlie Wessex. Her mother was the sitting judge for the county." Was she the one that died? Rayne asked him. "Yes, that's her. She and you were given the wrong test, as was one other nurse. Needless to say, she didn't do nearly as well as you two did. And as I said, you are a qualified physician. More than qualified if you were to ask me."

She didn't know what to say. Had no idea how she had managed to not just pass her test, but one that was well above her head. Thinking of the questions that had bothered her, she realized she had questioned herself about the test and how well she was going to do on it. It had been difficult but apparently not as bad as she'd thought. Something occurred to her, and she looked at Mr. Elliot.

"You're going to be still short-staffed with nurses. I can fill in for that if you need me to." He said he'd not do that to a fine doctor such as herself. "But you're short-staffed."

"We are. We will be, I guess, but this is going to put a nice shot in our arms as a hospital. While I know you didn't come from here, you're a doctor that was at this hospital. That will have nurses coming here in droves." She supposed there was that. "And when Charlie gets back from her leave, she has told me that she's decided to live in her mother's condo and work here. Like you, she wanted to have the small-town feel of working. As a doctor too. I'm just so thrilled about this I could dance a little jig."

He did just that. Standing up behind his desk,

Mr. Elliot danced around the room until he got to her. Pulled from her chair, she handed AJ to Wats, and he watched them dancing. It was cause for celebration, she thought. She was a doctor.

Going back to work was harder than it had been before. Questions were floating around in her mind that she wanted to ask someone. But with her still being on duty, she knew that now was not the time to find answers. It was like trying to hide her love for Wats or her daughter.

Sitting at one of the gurneys, she started just speaking to the little boy that had come in while she'd been upstairs until she realized his cut was much worse than it should have been for a cut from a piece of wire.

"I cut myself like this one time. I had to get twelve stitches in my arm. How many do you think you're going to need?" He didn't speak, but he did look at the woman that was with him. Rayne did too. "Do you know if he's had a tetanus shot or not?"

"I don't know anything but that he comes yelling at me that he's cut himself, and I bring him here. His regular doctor don't seem to be taking anybody today." She huffed. "This kid ain't mine, but my boyfriend's. He's going to be powerfully pissed off when he finds out I had to bring him in here. If not for the nosey neighbor threatening to call the cops if I didn't, I'd be at home watching my shows and shit."

The boy's entire body stiffened when the woman spoke. Rayne wasn't sure if it was the threat of his father or the woman, but she was going to make sure he was safe. Her mind was a jumble of things she had to do, and it wasn't until the curtain came back and Abby stuck her head into the room that she felt like she was going to be all right.

"This is Abby. She's the clerk that checks on things like that. If you'd not mind telling her his name, she can check the records to see if he's had all his shots up to date. Also, she'll need his father's name and address." The woman, who hadn't given her name on the paperwork in front of her, smiled. "I'd like to check it out if you don't mind. He may well be sicker if he's not had this shot."

Rayne was afraid to leave the little boy. Abby seemed to realize that too, asking the woman to come with her. She went with Abby but wasn't the least bit happy about it. Before she left the room, however, she looked at the little boy and said he'd better not be lying to anyone. She'd know.

As soon as she thought they were far enough away from the cubicle, Rayne smiled at him. Asking his name, he told her that they called him Mistake, and sometimes Shithead.

"Well, I'm sure you have a better name than that, don't you?" He nodded at her and then looked around before whispering his name. "All right, Louis. Why don't you tell me how you really hurt your arm. I can't stitch this closed until I'm sure it's not going to be infected."

"I don't lie." She said she knew that about him. "Dad tried to cut it off this morning on account of me having a glass of milk when he didn't say I could. I was really hungry. And I thought he was gone for the day when he come back and slapped me around. Then when Brenda told him I was a little thief and that I needed to be taught a lesson, he said he'd cut off my hand so I'd not be able to steal again. Don't tell them I told you. Please?"

"I won't." She hated that the child was so afraid. "I'm going to call another doctor in to see how many stitches we need to put in. You can trust him, Louis. He's a good man."

"I don't trust nobody, ma'am." That tugged at her heart so much that she had to look away in order to reach for the little device around her neck that would call anyone that she needed. She had noticed that Wats had his on when he'd been in the office with her.

"You miss us already? I'm still here if you need to have — Something is going on." She explained to him, not alarming Louis, that she had a patient that needed stitches. She asked him to come to her now, please. "I can do that. I have my father with me. Would it be all right if he were to come with me?"

"Yes. That would be wonderful." She smiled at Louis. "You'll like Mr. Wilkerson. He's a good man too. He'll have our daughter with him."

She didn't have to wait long for not only Wats to join her but also her father-in-law and Cooper. The man with them was one of the officers on the force and seemed to be off duty, as he was dressed in jeans and a shirt. She introduced Louis to them all, not telling him that Cooper was a cop. As soon as she showed them the cut on Louis's arm, Cooper stepped out, saying he'd return. Brenda returned just as he left them.

"What the fuck are you doing now? Having a tea party? I need him to get his ass home before his daddy shows up. He's going to be mad enough that I had to waste my time as it is." She put out her fist and told Louis he'd better have not been a bad boy. "Come on then. I guess you'll have to deal with it bleeding all the time. Get your ass in gear."

Before she could get out of the emergency department, three cruisers pulled into the lot with their lights and sirens on. Brenda slapped Louis hard enough to have him falling backward, and she took off running.

"I don't think she's going to get too far. Not with her slippers falling off and her pants that tight. Do you suppose she went to a store called 'I have no clue how to dress when I leave home, and I don't care'?" The police caught up with Brenda just as she was heading down the street. "You did good, honey. One more abuser off the streets is just what this town needed."

Louis was taken back to where he'd been before Brenda hit him. After examining him from head to toe, she found several more injuries that varied in the date given to him as well as types. Admitting him so that he could get some proper care, she was making sure he was in a room when the boy's father showed up to be stitched up too. Apparently, he didn't care for the police showing up and taking him away from his shows either.

"Mr. Sloan, it seems like you've had a busy morning." He told her to fuck off. "Yes, that's a good thing to say to someone that is going to put a needle in your arm."

"You ain't putting anything in my arm but sewing shit. I ain't having you drug me all up so you can do shit to me." She wondered what kind of "shit" he thought she was going to do to him when he growled at her. "You hear me? Just sew me up, and I'll be on my way. With my kid."

Rayne thought she was a little too excited about putting stitches in his arm and head without giving him anything for the pain first. Not giving him anything to numb the pain of her stitching him up was going to be quite painful, she thought. Taking several deep breaths, she let them out slowly before she opened her kit up and began to work. First, his arms, which needed four places stitched up, then his head. He'd already refused X-rays.

"Your little boy was pretty cut up." The man jerked from her needle when she pushed it through the skin. "You have to sit still, or this is going to take a lot longer than necessary."

"It hurts." She asked him if he wanted her to numb it. "Sure. I guess so. Not a lot, though. I want to have all my facilities when I leave here."

She thought that correcting him would be stupid. "As I was saying, your son, he was hurt pretty badly. He'll need to take better care that he doesn't climb trees in the future. Brenda might not be there to make sure he's not hurt more seriously." He laughed as the medication flowed through his veins. "Is that better?"

"Oh yeah." He laid this head back on the chair he was in. "Brenda hates him. Me too, but since his mom ran off a few years ago, I had to take care of him. Don't know what I'd have done if Brenda didn't care for him while I nap. He's a noisy little fuck."

"Why do you keep him if you hate him? I mean, there are all kinds of services that will make sure he gets to a good place." He told her how he got himself a check each month for him. "Oh. I guess I didn't think about that."

He opened one eye and looked at her. "You ain't going to tell me to get a job? Most people think it's easy being lazy. It ain't. I have to be thinking up new ways all the time to get myself out of doing shit." She asked him if he had ever worked. "Long time ago. But I got fired when I was caught napping on the job. Tell me this—how come they expect you to be at work at eight in the damned morning, and they don't let you take a couple of little snoozes along the day? I just couldn't do it."

Saying nothing, she watched him out of the corner of her eye. Cooper had told her to let him do the talking, and he might say something that would get his ass into trouble. The police were recording them, using the camera system that was in every cubicle of the emergency department. More police were at the house now, examining the blood and other items around the place. He also told her that the place looked like it was a dumping ground. Not hoarding, he told her, but just trash piled up all over the place.

"I did have me a sweet deal once. This guy gave me a hundred bucks for stealing shit off cars that were just sitting around. It was easy money until he got his ass caught." Rayne asked him if that was something he considered hard work. "Nah. I mean, I guess it is hard work, but it was fun ripping people off."

"I see. I'm going to work on the other cut now. How are you holding up?" He said he was fine but could use a little more juice." Calling for a nurse, she received a little more numbing medication and put it in his arm. "Better?"

"Yeah, that's the shit right there." She wondered if he was ever going to talk about the boy. That's what she wanted to get him on, abuse. "Where is that dumbass anyway? Brenda said she'd have him at the house before I woke up."

"He's been X-rayed for some broken ribs and some other injuries he must have gotten from falling." Sloan laughed. "Why do you find it funny that he is hurting?"

"The kid knows better than to say a word about how he gets himself beat up. I tell you, he's a lot more fun to knock around now that he's older." She stared at him. "Come on. You have to know he's no more fallen out of a tree than I'm a good person. He's a little thief that gets into the shit I pay for. I was going to teach him a lesson about that, but the neighbor came over and started screaming at me about the noise and shit."

"What did you do to him?" He seemed almost proud of the fact that he'd tried to cut his arm off. Sloan went into great detail about how he'd had Brenda hold Louis down while he used a butcher knife to try to cut his hand off. "Why would you not just give him a glass of milk? I mean, he's a growing boy and needs it."

"He ain't gonna be around much longer if he don't behave himself and stay out of shit that don't belong to him." Sloan laughed a little as she bent her head over her task. Letting him see her fury right now would not help Louis. "You sure are easy to talk to. I mean, I'd not say shit if we were being recorded or something. There are laws about that shit."

"About what shit? Recording you? I don't know if you saw them or not, but there are signs all over this place that tells you that you're being recorded." He shook his head and told her that was just signs they put up for people to think on it. "You believe that?"

"Sure. Them things are expensive, and I know

that this hospital ain't got the money like the big ones do. I mean, just look at what you got on. It says doctor on it. We both know that ain't something that is going to happen. Women are nurses. Men are doctors." He laughed again. She'd forgotten that she'd put on her new lab coat when she'd left the offices upstairs. "I got me one of them recording things at the house. When I'm in the mood, I sometimes replay some of the shit that I did during the day. That's how I know Mistake was into my milk. It was right there for everyone to see."

She heard a scuffle on the other side of the curtain, and then the curtain was pushed back. Cooper was standing there with a big smile on his face and his gun pointed at Sloan. He asked her if she wouldn't mind backing away from the man.

"Mr. Albert Sloan, you're under arrest for the attempted murder of Louis Sloan."

Rayne backed out of the room as Sloan's rights were read to him. Wats was right here with AJ, and he handed her the baby while he held her in his arms.

"You did a good job in there. I would have murdered him when he told me that he was lazy." She told him she'd been terrified that he'd not admit to what he'd done to the little boy. "I've gone up to check on Louis. He's in a room now, and they have him hooked up to an IV to help with his malnutrition. AJ was entertaining him while I was there. He's going into the system unless we take him with us. What do you think?"

"That's a silly question. Of course, we'll take him home with us when he's ready." Wats kissed her on the forehead, and she laid her head on his chest again. "He's so afraid, Wats. Do you think he'll trust us someday?"

"Yes. If for no other reason than we've not hurt AJ. He was checking her for marks when I was in the room with him. He was trying his best to be slick about it, but Louis did strip her down faster than my dad did when he looked her over." She laughed. "Brenda has been arrested, and now that Albert is going to jail, the police will go into the house and find whatever they can to keep the two of them in jail. Finding out about the recording devices was brilliant. I think Cooper nearly wet himself when he confessed to recording his beatings of the little guy."

"I just want to go up and check on Louis and make sure he gets a good dinner, then I'm going to take a nap. I don't want to leave him here, but I also am dragging right now and need a nap." He told her he'd stay with Louis tonight. "Thank you so much. As much as I'd like to stay too, I'm exhausted. Stress will do that for you."

"I can stay." She'd forgotten that Wesley was there with Wats. "In fact, I'd love to do it for you. Wats told me you might be taking him home to live with you too, and I think as his future grandpa, I should make sure I get to know him. Don't you think?"

She kissed him on the cheek and told him she loved him. Wesley just blushed and told her that he dearly loved her as well. As he walked away, rubbing his cheek where she'd kissed him, Rayne suggested that they order the two of them pizza so they could share it over getting to know each other. He told her he'd take care of it.

After putting AJ in her car seat, she got into the car too. Closing her eyes, she thought she was the luckiest person in the world—a home, husband— soon to be anyway—as well as children. There wasn't much else she could wish for.

~*~

Charlie decided she was going to keep the condo for a while anyway. It was close enough to the hospital that she could walk should she want. It was paid for, and the furniture wasn't that bad. While her mom had had an eclectic taste in furniture, it would suit her.

Going through the mail that had piled up

while she was gone, Charlie found her mother's death certificate, as well as some things that she could take care of right away. Wats had been nice enough to only keep the mail for her and toss out all the flyers that her mom had gotten. Today she was going to go to the bank and see what was there that needed her attention.

Her mother's bank account had been frozen when she was shot. Going there this morning, she was going to be able to get into the account and open up one for herself to use to take care of unpaid bills, as well as anything else that hadn't been cared for before her mother was killed.

Leaning back on the couch she'd removed the plastic from when she arrived last night, she thought about her mom. Mom was a good person. Everyone that Charlie had spoken to since her mom's death had only good things to say about her. Even people that had been before her in court said she'd been fair and had worked around things so as not to hurt their families when it was unnecessary.

Charlie knew her mom had taken to heart one of the men she had sentenced. She made it so he only spent time in the cell at night after his sitter came for his three children. As he was working too, she told him so long as he didn't miss a day of work, she'd work with him. There was no reason for the man to lose his job over a few parking tickets that he'd not had the money to pay. She was generous like that to a lot of people, Charlie had come to understand.

Getting up to see what sort of foodstuff she was going to have to toss, she found a note from Abby Wilkerson. In it, she told her how the house had been gone over, and anything that was perishable had been either donated or tossed out. She had also made sure Charlie had a few staples to use until she was able to fill the cupboards again. The Wilkersons were nice people too. She'd come to depend on them over the last several weeks.

While her eggs cooked on the stove, she thought about her being a physician. While she didn't think she'd learned anything in her classes that was on the test, she was able, from having read a great deal, to get the right answers when the situations were spelled out for her. A doctor. Her mom would have been so very proud of her. She would also have gotten a big kick out the way it had happened.

When the phone rang in the living room, Charlie didn't bother going to answer it. She'd not given her mom's number out, so whoever it was, they wanted her mom, not her. Her cell phone rang just as the phone stopped ringing in the other room. She smiled when Wats's face appeared.

"I tried to call the house phone. Silly of me to think you'd answer it. Anyway. I'd like to invite you over to have dinner with my new little family." He told her how he and Rayne had adopted a little girl and that they were working to keep a six year old little boy too. "We're growing by leaps and bounds here. Also, I wanted to talk to you about what you're going to do about working. Now that you've finished school, I need a partner. Rayne is going to stay on at the hospital. She might be better off there than working with me. I don't know that we'd get too much done anyway."

"How will this work if I say yes to working with you? I know little to nothing about partnerships." He said his dad was an attorney, and if she wanted to ask legal questions, he could answer them. "Isn't one of your brothers an attorney too? North, I think."

"Yes. He's working with his dad and uncles. They are all taking a lot of pro-bono cases and enjoying the work. North is working with the city too. Did I tell you his dad is running for mayor? He's getting a lot of things done around town already. I think he'll be a shoo-in for the job when the voting comes up." She told him her mom had mentioned it. "Yeah, he had to apply to run, and she helped him with the paperwork. She might have fast-tracked it a bit for him. She was a wonderful woman, Charlie.

I hope you know everyone is sad to see her gone."

"Me too." She looked around the condo. "Do you know if I have any kinds of rights to this place? I know it's paid for, with the exception of the dues. But I'd like to paint a bit and get new carpets. These are showing their age a bit. Not to mention some work is needed in the kitchen area."

"Since you own it, you can do what you wish to the inside. I'm sure I don't have to tell you that you can't do something illegal there. But Mars told us so long as the yards were kept up, he didn't care what a person might do to the inside to make it their own. My dad wanted an air-conditioner in his bedroom. He likes his room to be freezing when he sleeps, something I guess he wasn't able to do when Mom was alive." She said she liked a warm bed and a cold room too. "You would love sleeping with—never mind. You don't need to sleep with Booker to know that the two of you have something in common."

Her laughter felt good. She'd not had a lot of opportunities of late to think of something as funny, and this was just what she needed. After they made arrangements for him to call North for her so he'd be with her when the will was read, she laid back down on the couch.

Wats was a good friend. All the Wilkersons

were that she'd met so far. They were kind yet firm. They didn't intrude where they shouldn't, and they would give someone their last penny if they thought someone needed it more than they did.

Her cell phone rang then, and it was Wats again. However, when she answered the phone, he told her his name was Mars. He asked her what she wanted done to the condo and that there were contractual things that he did yearly for the place.

"Your mom didn't want us to do anything to the place because she said she was rarely there. According to the notes I have on your address, it's due for not just all new carpets, but an upgrade to the kitchen. She skipped that one three times." They both laughed when she told him Mom didn't cook. "Since the place is paid off, you can pick what carpet you want in the place, and since we're going to be doing that, we can paint all the rooms while we're at it. Mom wanted people to be happy in their homes so they'd stay longer. Also, she said that since people stayed so long, we saved money on advertising when there was an empty spot."

"I'd like that, please. An overhaul to the place." He suggested another route they could go. "You mean I could actually trade in this place for another one? That would be nice. The memories here, there aren't a lot of them, but the ones I have are painful. What sort of deal can you make me?"

"I can give you the house numbers to the ones that are fully updated. Some of them have more bedrooms, but that won't make much of a difference if you take one of them instead. I have two that have four bedrooms and one that has five. If I were you, I'd take the five. It's sitting alone in the street, and since it's so big, you're not sharing any walls with anyone. It's the only house we have in this area." She said she'd take it. "Good. You'll be closer to town, as well as the other shops that are finally getting filled out in town. If you let me know when you'd like to go there, I can meet you there with the keys. Anytime is good for me."

"Now?" Mars said that was good with him. He was headed out the door now. "I'm guessing you don't live here anymore. That big house on the main drag, I heard it's being renovated now."

"Yes. It's worse than your mom's condo. It's been literally centuries since anyone updated even the paint in the place." She asked him if he thought he'd enjoy living in the house. "I think so. Abby and I are going to make memories of our own. Have laughter with all my cousins and their wives. It's been tough, I will admit that, but Mom left me in a good place, and I'm doing everything I can to make sure she'd still be proud of me."

"I'm sure she is."

She told him she was leaving now and got directions to find the house. It was exciting for her to be able to start fresh and still be close to friends. While she didn't know all the Wilkerson men, she knew that all the ones she did know were about as kind as they could be to her. And Mom had loved them to pieces too.

Chapter 8

Booker couldn't wait for the end of the term. He had so much going on at his condo that he wasn't sure he was ever going to see the light of day again. Then there was the move to his new home. Why did he buy such a huge assed house? He'd been asking himself the same question for days now.

Booker looked up when he heard his name being called. It was Brandon. He wanted them to have dinner together.

"I have about six thousand reports I have to read and grade. Then after that, the school is asking for next year's plan. I don't even know what I'm going to be doing tomorrow, much less next year." He put his paperwork into his briefcase and looked at his friend and cousin. "You know what? Fuck it. I would love to have dinner with you."

They ended up at their favorite place. The steakhouse on campus, usually very busy in the fall, had already gotten the parent rush over with, and it was mostly just him and Brandon there. He asked his cousin what he'd been doing.

"I have three designs I'm working on at the same time. They aren't even related to each other." Booker asked him if it was harder that way. "Usually not. When I get stuck on one of them, I can work on the other two to clear my mind. But here lately, it's lost all of its appeal. Most everything has. How about you? I'm sorry about your mom. Sort of."

"They're all gone, had you heard?" Brandon told him he'd heard it from his dad. "We're none of us going to miss them, I don't think. I find myself missing Aunt Holly more than I ever did my mother. Dad, he's happy. He has a date tonight, and he is as excited as I get when I have a new class starting."

"My dad has been working around town with Uncle Clayton. If he gets to be mayor, he's going to have so much help from his brothers that I wouldn't doubt that the town will be upgraded within his first few weeks in office. Did you hear he's running on a platform that says, whatever Mayor Caldwell says he'll do, Uncle Clayton is going to actually do it. I laughed my ass off the first time I read that on one of his signs." He asked him if it was slander. "Only if it's not true. Caldwell isn't getting anything done around the town. Last weekend Mrs. Orr fell on one of the sidewalks, and not only did Uncle Clayton help her to get a new sidewalk in front of her home, but he did some of the work himself. Not for show either — he was digging right along with the crew. That's what this town needs. A member of the town out where people can see him."

They spoke about the town as they waited on their salads. Booker loved things hot and spicy, while Brandon was a little on the timid side when it came to spice. Booker's salad had sriracha sauce on it and then a bottle of it on the side. He loved it on his salad as much as Brandon hated it.

After their salads were cleared away, Brandon got serious. He wanted advice. Not sure how he could help him, Booker listened to what he had to say until he finished. Actually, he was glad to hear that someone else was thinking what he'd been thinking and let out a long breath before he spoke.

"I don't want to work anymore either. I feel, just like you do that I've been forced to work at something I don't enjoy for a long time." Brandon asked him if he hated teaching. "Not hate. That's too strong a word for it. But I'm ready to see some things before I get too old to enjoy them. I've never been to an amusement park by myself. Holly took us to those things, but now I want to see them again. Perhaps with a date this time. I don't know. I've been a college professor for ten long years now, and I want a break."

"I've been an engineer for that long, and I'm sick of it. Not just sick, but I think I've grown to hate my job." Booker asked him what he wanted to do, if anything. "Like you, I want to see places. Also, I want to work on game designs. I've been doing a little of that on the side, but there are times when I just want to walk away. That's hard for me to do."

"Because we've had it beat into us that we are to work where we're told and not deviate from that plan at all." Booker had a thought. "I'm going to turn in my resignation tomorrow. I'll work to the end of the term for them, then I'm done. I'm going to be my own man."

"Damn it, so am I." They had a glass of wine with their dinner, something that he rarely did, and had fun the rest of the night. "Wats told me about your home, Book. Are you ready to get moved in?"

Booker told him that he was pretty much moved in now. "Come over to the house and watch some television with me. I'll show you around. When I get out of working, I think I'll devote some time to just being a lazy man. I don't think I've ever done much of that." He asked him if he had a place to sit. "More than enough, actually. I've emptied out my storage lockers and filled out the house nicely. I even had paper napkins in the cabinet."

Something that their mothers would never allow them to use. Booker thought of being at Aunt Holly's and how they'd sometimes use paper towels when she didn't have any napkins. She had given them a taste of a life that they'd never had at home — a good time, as with nothing ever having to be expensive or top name.

As he walked through the house, he remembered when he'd gotten each piece and told Brandon about it. Holly had turned him on to them, and the two of them would go to them to have fun. She did something with each of them. Brandon's passion had been going to plays with her. He was going to do that as well — see some plays and go to the movies once in a while.

The house looked good if he did say so himself. He had even gotten some nice dishes that he had put away himself, as well as cloth napkins. He wasn't opposed to using them, but he also knew there wasn't a reason to have them while enjoying a slice of pizza. Asking Brandon if he wanted to stay over, he took him to one of the bedrooms that were complete. The bathroom had extras in it, such as toothpaste and other items for guests.

"I have to get myself a washer and dryer, however. I never wanted to get one at an auction. Aunt Holly said if I didn't use it right away, I might be buying a pig in a poke." They laughed again, and Booker was feeling better all the time. "The sheets and mattresses are new, so you don't have to worry about those. So are the towels. I do have a stack of old ones, but I'm going to be using them in the garage or the barn. I've not decided what I'm going to be doing with the barn yet, but I'm sure it'll come to me."

"There is an auction tomorrow. I'm sure you've seen it." Booker asked him where it was. "About an hour from here. I thought you and I could take a trip there to see about me getting a start on my home that I don't have yet."

"All right." They were going to leave early in the morning and be there in time to look things over. Booker was excited to be spending time with Brandon. "I have a few pieces that I don't have room for if you want them. You can even store your things in my locked place. Or the barn. As I said, I don't know what I'm going to be doing out there as yet, and this way, you can get as much as you need."

"Thanks. I think I'll take you up on that. Lord knows I have enough boxes at the condo to fill out a couple of rooms. When Dad told me to get what I wanted from the house before he sold it, I did just that. Most of it was from my room, and then the staff packed up things from the attic that I hadn't any idea was up there." Booker asked him what it was. "Believe it or not, the staff saved all my baby things. Report cards and whatnot. When I was there to get my clothes from the closet, they told me that they knew Mom wouldn't have kept it, so they did. Lots of things that brought back lots of memories."

"That's nice." He asked Brandon if he had a house in mind yet. "I did look over the list you sent me about the foreclosure homes. I have to admit, I would never have dreamed there were that many around here. There are two that I'm going to have a look at on Monday. I might not buy anything yet—I'm in no hurry to get something just to get something—but I will have something soon."

"Take Wats with you. That man can wheel and deal better than anyone I've worked with. Just the other day, he told me he got four buildings in the downtown area for a steal. I looked it up. He did. He paid a thousand dollars for four buildings. He told me even though he was going to have to take one of them down, he still made out well. Abby is going to use one of them for a studio for her and Amy to use to take pictures. The other place they had turned out to be a bust. It needed all new wiring, and that was well beyond what the building was worth." Brandon said he'd do that. "We're all getting wives. Do you suppose we'll be in that group of old married people too?"

"More than likely." He then asked Brandon if he'd met Louis. "I did. I heard that he came home this morning, so I went by and gave him some gifts. The kid was afraid to open the package until Rayne assured him she had no intentions of selling it off."

"Poor kid. And I have to tell you, I'm completely in love with AJ. Have you seen Uncle Wesley around the kids? He's in heaven. Having so much fun with the kids that I swear he's ten years or so younger." Brandon said his dad was thrilled with AJ too. He loved being a great uncle. "That's right. I forgot about that."

They wandered around the house until they ended up in the living room. There wasn't much on the television this time of night, so they opted to just let it play in the background as they brought up fond memories. Most of them were of when they were all together, and they also talked about how much they were enjoying being around their dads. Booker said he and his dad were having a wonderful time getting to know one another.

"It's been really comforting to know my dad

is trying so hard to be the man he should have been. I didn't say that to him—he told me that the other night when he was here. Also, and this is something I think all of us feel, our fathers are feeling better just knowing they are free of their ex-wives. I know that sounds terrible, but—"

"No, it doesn't sound terrible. It's the truth." Booker asked him how he felt about them all being gone. "Nothing. I don't feel anything. It's as if someone told me that a great uncle I never met has passed away. There hasn't been any feelings for my mother or the others for a very long time. I think since well before I left home."

"That is sad. Not on our part, but theirs. If you ask me, they're the ones that lost out. Not only did they never get to know any of us, but they missed out on knowing Aunt Holly too." He realized they were talking about something they should be avoiding right now. Sadness wasn't going to interfere in his life as much anymore. "Anyway, we should get going about seven in the morning. We can stop on the way and get some breakfast too. The auction starts at ten, so that will give us a good hour to look around and make notes on things."

"I'm excited about this new venture, Book. I swear, I've never enjoyed things as much as I do today. I think it has to do with knowing that no one is going to be hurt or hurt me and that I'm going to do something I want for a change." Booker agreed. "All right. Good night, buddy. And thanks for being there for me. I love you."

"And I love you, Brandon. But let's not be mushy about it." They were both laughing as they parted ways in the hall. Booker set his alarm on his phone and laid down. Closing his eyes with a smile on his face, he thought of one more thing. "I miss you, Aunt Holly. Very much. But I'm moving on now. Thanks to you, I can do that."

~*~

Charlie wasn't sure what the hell she was doing. Not just here, but what she was to do if she wanted to bid on something. Abby and Amy had talked her and Rayne into coming up to this auction today to fill out their homes. She thought they had nice homes, but what did she know about being wealthy? Not a single thing.

The man she'd been sort of following was helping another man in things that he should bid on and how much. She had also learned not to take the first amount that the auctioneer put out there. It was only a starting point.

"Hello." She looked around when the man she was following spoke to her. "You haven't any idea what you're doing, do you?"

"Nope. I will admit I'm in well over my head. Like I need all kinds of things for this house I'm going to live in, but I haven't any idea how to go about it. Like, this table here. I love it. But I don't know what would be a good price to bid or how to even make that happen." He asked her if she had a number yet. "Yes. I got that when we first arrived. Abby told me about that."

"Abby? You're here with Abby Wilkerson?" She nodded, and the man laughed. "Well, isn't this a small world. I'm her cousin-in-law, Booker Wilkerson. I'm here with my cousin, Brandon."

"Will you help me?" He said he'd love to. "Good. First thing, this table. What is a good price to pay? I don't want to get caught up in the bidding and forget that I'm on a budget, somewhat."

"It's not old if that's what you're thinking." She asked him how he could tell that. "Look around at all the other pieces out here. What is the one thing they have in common? I know you can see it, but it never occurred to you yet."

She knew he wasn't talking about the age of the piece. To her, they all looked like they'd been around a long time. Then she noticed a few things she'd not before. Looking at Booker, she smiled.

"Someone has taken the time to dust this piece. Why would they do something like that to a piece that's just a table?" He told her. "I guess I can see that. Polish it up so that it's more appealing to someone. Eye catching, I guess you could call it. So it will more than likely go a little high when it's probably just a table that isn't going to last all that long. Thank you."

"You're so very welcome. Also, you should never, if you can help it, linger too long when looking at a piece. That gives away that you're interested. Sort of casually look at something, then look around while keeping an eye on other people that look at it. You can figure out your competition that way." She giggled. Charlie told him he was wonderful for helping her. "I'm enjoying myself too, so it's good for us both."

They walked around together for the next half hour. Booker pointed out things she could bid on and how much she should go. He told her when she asked him if he'd help her when the bidding started that he'd love to, but he also had to help Brandon.

"Oh, I'm sorry. You did tell me you were here with him. You have given me a lot to go on, and I appreciate that." He told her he wasn't going to leave her. "But what about Brandon? Won't he be upset?"

"Right now, I don't care. You're much prettier than he is. Plus, he's hanging out with Abby. Who is, I might say, good at this too." The announcement was made that bidding would begin in five minutes. "Something else you might want to do when you go to an auction is to find out who the auctioneer is and make a mental note to watch how he does things. I ask where he might be starting when he begins and also if he will have a second auctioneer selling in another area. There is only the one person here until noon. Then they're going to sell the house and land around it. But he's going to start with the box lots. Those are the boxes of stuff that they deemed not worth too much, and they're getting rid of it. I find a lot of good things in those sort of boxes."

"Like what?" They were headed to the box-lots area now. "Oh, I understand now. They're literally boxes of just stuff. I think getting a couple of those would be a blast just to go through and see what junk you can find." She laughed.

"You'd be amazed at the things my Aunt Holly and I found in them." She was enjoying herself so much that she nearly forgot that they were here for a purpose. "Okay, remember what I said. Stick with the price you want to pay for it, and don't take the first amount he puts out there."

She didn't want anything in the box he was trying to sell off, and neither did anyone else, it seemed. As the bidding didn't generate even a buck, he added another box, then another. The box next, the one with the office things in it, was something she was interested in. When Booker leaned down and whispered in her ear, all thoughts of bidding flew out of her head.

"You'll have to take them all—remember that when you buy a bunch of boxes." She nodded, and when the auctioneer said a dollar, she raised her hand. While she had no idea what was in the boxes that she'd want, the office equipment appealed to her. Someone put their hand up, but he was only waving at someone across from him. The auctioneer asked him to conduct his conversations elsewhere and looked at her.

"You won, missy." She jumped for joy. Laughing, she went to the auctioneer and hugged him before she realized what she was doing. Telling him it was her first auction and bidding, he laughed with her. "Well, I'm glad you came here today. Thanks for the hug too."

When she started to go for her boxes, Booker told her to wait. No one would bother with them. He purchased the next lot of eight boxes, and she bought two more at the end that were filled with glasses, as well as wine glasses that she really liked. The two of them, she thought, had gotten a lot of junk with their stuff.

They started a pile by one of the trees. Booker even purchased a chair so she'd have something to sit in under the tree. When the rest of the boxes were sold off, her buying two more lots for a total of ten, the other Wilkersons joined them. They had twenty minutes before the bidding began on the furniture.

"Are you having fun?" She told Abby she was having too much fun, she thought. She didn't know how she was going to get everything in her car. "Don't worry about that. I called Mars, and he's going to rent one of those hauling things to bring our stuff home in. I missed the box lots, but I see you didn't. Would you mind if I went through them with you? Just to look at the things people consider junk?"

"I'd love that." Booker bought her lunch, as well as two bottles of water. The house, it seemed, wasn't selling for much, and she watched Booker when he decided it would be a good investment. Charlie moved closer to him when he started to tense up when the bidding started. "You can do this."

He only glanced at her, but she could see that he was happy she'd said that. His face not only relaxed, but he wasn't fisting his hands either. Putting her smaller hand into his much larger one, she felt like she was centered. It was a strange way to feel with only just meeting the man.

Booker bought the house, or so they all thought. Since it had gone well under what they should have gotten for the place, the auctioneer had to speak to the family. Booker kissed the back of her hand when he was asked to wait until the auctioneer returned.

"Thank you." She told him he was welcome and that he had calmed her as well. "We'll go to the furniture next. Are you ready for that?"

"I believe I am." She watched as the household things were brought out where the boxes had been. The big bed that came with several pieces of furniture caught her eye. Admiring it from a distance, she watched as others went over the stuff like they were searching for something special in it. "Are they serious about buying it for that price? I've heard that some of them are only willing to go to less than a hundred dollars. That seems cheap to me."

"They're putting that out there so that others around, like you, would hear it. They want you thinking it's not worth all that much. But I've seen it in the bedroom before you got here, and it's well worth a thousand or more. It's very old and made of mahogany. It looks to me like it might have been handmade right here on the property. That is a really good piece." She nodded but didn't go near the bedroom set. She didn't have the kind of money that would justify her paying that much for just a bedroom suite. Charlie did have her inheritance, but she was saving that for a rainy day. Booker laughed when she told him that. "My aunt would have told you that there are forever going to be rainy days, and you won't be able to save for all of them. What you should do is make each day count so that when the rainy day does come, you have your comfort in the things you did when you had the money and time."

"I think I might have liked your aunt." Booker kissed her then. Just a quick kiss on the mouth. "That was nice. Booker, I'm beginning to like you a great deal. Is that odd?"

"No. It's the way it should be. Come on, let's get us a place to bid on the things that we want. If you want the bedroom suite, then you get it. I'll even help you pay for it if it comes to being close to your limit." It didn't bother her that he was willing to do that. For some reason, it seemed right that they purchased the set together. Shaking her head at the nonsense in it, she moved to the group of people that had gathered around not just the bedroom suite but the table and chairs that had been brought out as well. "That is beautiful. Don't you think?"

"It is." A thought popped into her head in that moment. Of him sitting at one end of the table and her at the other, with people seated down either side with children in their arms. The thought, or vision, was so vivid that her breath caught when she realized this was their children and grandchildren. "Booker, something isn't right about this."

"I know." She had a feeling he did know, and she nodded too. "We'll figure things out when we get back home. All right. Today, let's just fill out our home."

She nearly missed bidding on the bedroom suite. Her mind was filled with words like home. Our. Even the vision of them and a large family. When Booker poked her in the ribs, she looked at the auctioneer when he started the bidding out at six thousand dollars.

When he got back down to a hundred dollars, a man in the crowd behind her said, "Here." She didn't turn and glare at him as she wanted to do but kept her eye on the man doing the fast-talking. Booker told her to wait to see where it went and if anyone was going to bid with them. When he told her now, she lifted her hand up to bid one-fifty.

The man behind her moved up to where they were standing. She saw him out of the corner of her eye and didn't like that he was staring at her. When

Booker moved between the two of them, she felt better. The man started cursing quietly at first, then he started getting a little louder.

"Nothing is going to happen to you, love. All right? Just do what you're doing, and it'll be all right." Then the man shoved Booker into her. It wasn't a light push either. Both of them nearly tumbled to the ground. "Excuse me. You nearly knocked us down."

The man bumped Booker in the chest with his belly. Then he started talking to him in another language. While she had no idea what was being said, Booker did and was talking to the man calmly and without raising his fists up like the other man was.

"Hey. Hey now. What's all this about?" Booker told the auctioneer that the man had insulted his wife. Had called her a slut, and said that she only wanted the bed to entertain other men on. "He said that to you? What the hell — pardon me, ma'am — but what the hell is he being upset about? It's only an auction."

The man said something else, and Booker looked at the auctioneer. There were some very tense-filled moments there while neither of them spoke as the man went on and on about something. Not only did Abby join them, but all the Wilkersons stood up behind them.

"Mars, are you with this group?" He said he was. That this was his family. "This isn't right. Not to you or anyone in your family. But to be insulting like this to a pretty woman is just beyond what I think is right."

"I agree, Mr. Shadow." He asked the man to leave, and he just stood there, staring at her. Finally, when she'd had enough, she pushed her way in front of Booker, and he put his hands gently on her shoulders.

"You're a nasty bully." She asked Booker to translate for her. He said that he understood what she was saying. "You are the meanest man I've met. We were all having a good time until you had to get all up in arms about a bedroom suite. What is the matter with you? Don't you have any man—?"

The blow to her face knocked her back. She not only saw stars, but she was sick with the pain of it. Closing her eyes when it became too much for her, Charlie wondered what her mother would say to her now. She'd think it was funny, she'd bet. There were noises going on, cursing too, but in the end, she just let go. Letting the pain take her under so that she'd not feel it for a while.

Chapter 9

Wats was as pissed off as he'd ever been. Someone had actually hit a woman because she was bidding against him. Every time he thought about him hitting Charlie, he had to stop what he was doing and take a deep breath.

"This will go a good deal faster if you would just let your wife fix me up." He said he knew that, but he was safer in here. "Why? The guy was arrested, you told me."

"But I know where they took him." Charlie laughed, then moaned. "I'm sorry you were hurt. But if it's any consolation, you got the bedroom suite for nothing."

"Booker told me." She looked around, then back at him. "May I ask you a question? You don't have to answer, but please don't make fun of me.

All right?"

"Yes. But you should know that I don't lie. If you ask me something, you'd better be prepared for the answer. Ask me." She did. He had to think about his answer hard before he answered her. "You're worried that you're falling in love with my cousin? How is that something I'd make fun of you about?"

"I've only just met him today. I mean, literally today. He's kind and wonderfully sweet. He doesn't rush into things. Nor does he, and this is a biggy, treat me like I'm some sort of bimbo that he needs to protect." He laughed with her. "I suppose looking at me, you'd think I do need a protector. But he didn't shove me out of the way when I went to talk to the man. I know it was a stupid thing for me to do. I mean, I should have let someone handle it for me, but he didn't do anything."

"Actually, he did." She asked him what he was talking about. "My wife can't come here and take care of you because she's taking care of Booker. He has a broken wrist as well as needing stitches in both his lip and his hand. He knocked the man to his ass with one blow. He came up with a gun, believe it or not. But Booker didn't back down, he— Where are you going? I still need to stitch you up."

"Where is he?" Wats followed her, but not too closely. He could tell that she was pissed off, and he didn't want to come between her and her anger. "Booker Wilkerson, where the hell are you?"

He yelled that he was here, so she went to find him. As soon as they entered the room he'd been put in, Wats cringed. It was going to take him longer to heal from his wounds than it would Charlie, of that he was sure. Charlie asked him if he had a brain injury that she needed to be made aware of.

"Not that I'm aware of, no." Wats noticed that everyone seemed to leave them alone except him and Rayne. He was staying for the fun—he had no idea why Rayne was. "I was mad that he hit you."

"I was too, but you should have let the police handle it when he pulled out a gun." Booker looked at him, then back at Charlie. She did the same but looked at Booker. "What? Something you're not telling me."

"He was going to kill you." Charlie looked at Wats again. At his nod, she turned to Booker again. "I was willing to let the police handle it. I was sure that if I started on him, I would have killed him. But he pulled out the gun with the intention of killing you. He announced to everyone that you were one dead slut."

Booker stood up and made his way to Charlie. When she went into his arms willingly, Wats asked if they could finish stitching them up. They didn't want the swelling to get too much before they could get that done.

"I missed getting that table for our house." Wats didn't say anything about what Charlie said, but he did glance at his own wife. "This is so unfair. My very first auction and I have to get next to some dummy head that had to ruin it all for me."

"They stopped the auction." Charlie asked Rayne what she meant. "No one here wanted to go on without you there. The police are still here, of course, but the others voted to wait to see if you were going to join them again. The people here, they're really impressed with the two of you."

"We didn't do anything." Wats told her what he'd seen. "Okay, we did take on a bully, but we wouldn't have had to if he'd been a nicer person. What did he say to you?"

Booker said it wasn't nice, and wanted to leave it at that. Wats was sure that Charlie was going to push it, but she laid down on the bed that Booker was on so she could be stitched up as well. It took them more time than it normally would have because the two of them were talking to each other. Wats thought he was seeing the first blossoms of love.

When they were released to go back to the auction, people cheered for them. A couple of women told Booker he could defend their honor anytime he wanted. It was embarrassing to him. Wats could tell. Everyone was good-natured about it, and the police asked if they could talk to the two of them when the auction was over. Wats was very proud of his family right then.

Mars said he'd bid for them, but Charlie declined. She said her fun had been delayed, and she wanted to get back into it now. But she kissed him on the cheek for being so sweet, and then she turned to the auctioneer, asking him if he was ready.

"Yes, ma'am, I am. I have to tell you, I was never so terrified in my life as when that man said he was going to kill you. I thought for sure my heart was gonna stop when that husband of yours just stood up and knocked his gun away. Goodness." Charlie thanked him. "My wife, she said she's going to be watching for you from now on. You surely do get the job done when someone is nasty to you."

There was some fun made when Charlie bid on the dining set. They teased them both about being careful not to bid against them. As was Booker's nature, he got a kick out of it and didn't anger. Wats only then realized it was the first time he'd truly ever seen his cousin pissed. He was usually one that would just walk away. This was a first for all of them today.

Not only did she win the dining set, but she also was able to bid and get two more bedroom suites. He wasn't sure, but he thought he'd found someone that loved auctions as much as Booker and Aunt Holly had. She was getting good at knowing when to stop, too.

As they were loading up the things on the truck Wats had gotten, Booker asked him for something for his headache. After checking him out, he told him he wanted some pictures of his head if he didn't mind. When he agreed, that worried him just a little, but Booker assured him it was only a headache. Uncle Josiah showed up just as the auction was coming to an end.

"There you are." Booker shook hands with the auctioneer and told him he ran a good auction. "You're a good man to have around. I don't suppose you have yourself a shop, do you? I mean, the way your missus was buy—"

"Missus?" Uncle Josiah looked around, then at his son. "Oh, yes. All right. But we do need to talk about some things later, son. All right?"

Uncle Josiah looked confused, but he wasn't going to embarrass them by asking questions now. Charlie asked him what he had in mind when the auctioneer asked about the shop.

"Well, you see all this stuff that people leave

behind? Some of it is worth a little bit. A lot of it they just leave behind because they've realized they don't have the room to take it with them. I need someone I can call on to come and pick it up for me, and I'll pay you to do it. It won't be a lot, mind you, but a couple of dollars a box should cover you coming and getting it. If you've got a mind to."

Booker looked at his dad. "Will you go into partnership with me, Dad? I've decided I've had enough of teaching for a while, and I want to do something different. With you." Uncle Josiah looked like he was going to cry, and Wats patted him on the back. "We just purchased a house that I think will be perfect for odds and ends. My wife here is a doctor now, so she can afford to keep me in pocket money."

"I'd love nothing more." While Wats didn't know what house Booker was referring to, everyone was happy all the way around. "But first, I'd like for you to get to the hospital. The police said they'd make sure that the bill was paid by that moron."

"Do you want this to start now, Mr. Shadow?" Wats had forgotten the man's name and was glad that Charlie knew it. "We have enough help here today to load this up if you want. I mean, if that's all right with the rest of you."

"I have a better idea." Mars looked at Booker,

then at him. "You go to the hospital with these two
and make sure they're all right. The rest of us will
do the clean-up and take it where you want."

"I bought this house. I think it will be perfect
for where we can start out." They began to take
the boxes and other things into the truck while he
and Rayne loaded the two of them up in his car. He
was beginning to worry about Booker, as he was
too agreeable to going. He was going to keep him
overnight just to make sure, no matter what the
X-ray told them.

The ride to the hospital was quiet. He could
hear Charlie and Booker talking to each other, but
they were too quiet for him to hear. When Rayne
took his hand into hers, he looked over at her.

"She loves him." Wats said he could see that
too. "I think he loves her as well. He surely has
taken a beating for her if he doesn't."

"They'll be all right, don't you think?" She
asked him if he was worried about Booker. "Yes.
He's not himself. I'm worried that there is something
more wrong with him. I only checked his head.
What if he was hurt elsewhere? I'm going to keep
them both overnight, even if I have to beat the two
of them into submission." Rayne agreed with him.
And that made him more worried than he'd been
before.

~*~

Rayne read the X-rays three times before she was satisfied with the results. Not that she was happy with what she saw, but she knew they were lucky that she and Wats had brought them into the hospital. Charlie had a concussion and two broken ribs, more than likely from falling over when hit. Wats joined her just as she was going to go see Charlie.

"He was shot. The shithead was shot, and he didn't say a word about it." Rayne asked how bad it was. "He was shot. Bad enough that I'm worried."

"You're worried because he's your relative. Tell me what you really think, like he's no relation to you." Wats said it was serious, but not that bad. "Good. She has a concussion. So getting them to stay will be easier since they'll both be here."

"I have him going into surgery now. I can't join him there, but I can be with him when he gets out. He also has a concussion and four broken ribs. I'm sure he's also got a couple of broken fingers." Rayne said he was a good man. "What do you mean? He was shot and didn't tell anyone."

"He didn't want to freak you out. Or, for that matter, Charlie." He'd not thought of that. "Would you have let them stay there had you known? I wouldn't have. But Charlie got to have a good time, and her day wasn't totally ruined by that man. Booker was a good man in being stoic and not worrying her or any of us too much."

"You know, he's always been like that. I remember once him having a broken hand during a football game." She asked how he'd gotten it. "He was the quarterback. I guess he was too good, and the other team thought they could take him out. But he played the rest of the game and even won before he let on that he was injured. I should have remembered that."

Rayne went to tell Charlie that she was spending the night. Wats told her that Booker was going to be fine but that he'd sustained a larger issue. Charlie had to threaten his life before he finally told her what had happened. She sat there for several moments without speaking, only to look at them with tears in her eyes.

"He said he loved me. We only met today, but it seems right. I don't know what to do about it. I mean, we only just met." Rayne asked if she loved him. "Yes. I don't know how that happened either, but knowing what he did for me today makes me love him all the more. Does that make sense to you?"

"Absolutely. It's the same thing for Wats and I." Rayne sent Wats on an errand while she sat on the side of the bed with Charlie. "He's going to be fine, you know. And if he won't behave, one of the others will sit on him until he does."

"Wats asked me to be his partner in his office. Are you going to be all right with that?" Rayne told her she was, that she was family now. "I guess I will be. Josiah, he was certainly confused. But he was really nice about not giving us up about the lie. It was nice, too, being called Mrs. Wilkerson."

"It is. Very nice. And you couldn't be joining a better family." Rayne called in the staff to make sure they started an IV for her, and told her that she'd let her know when Booker was out. Then when she left Charlie to her nurse, she stopped at the desk and asked if they could put Booker into the room with Charlie. "They'll be roaming the halls if you don't."

"We can arrange that, Dr. Wilkerson. My goodness, there are going to be a lot of you Wilkersons around here, aren't there? We'll have to make sure we use your initials, or we'll all be messed up." Rayne nodded and left to find Wats. It was the first time she'd been called Doctor Wilkerson by staff. It felt damned good.

As they waited for Booker to come out of surgery, Rayne made a couple of phone calls. One to her aunt to let her know where they were, and the second call to Josiah. He had asked her to call when they found out anything. He told her that he'd be right there. Wats went home to get Louis so that he could hang out with the others. He was becoming a wonderful part of the family quickly.

Rayne's phone rang, and she almost didn't answer it. Her aunt had called her several times over the last few days, and she wasn't ready to talk to her yet. But this time, armed with her anger that her newest family members had been hurt, as well as liking Charlie, she answered the phone with her title and Wilkerson.

"Where is Selma?" Rayne asked who it was, knowing full well that it was Aunt Becky. "Don't be a smart ass. Tell me where that sister of mine is. I have a mind to give her a piece of my mind."

"I'm sure you couldn't afford to give her any of your mind. You have seemed to lost your marbles anyway if you think that she's going to forgive you for treating her and me the way you did." Becky snorted. "You think I'm kidding? I'm not. I'm happy. I have children that I love and Aunt Selma to talk to when I need an adult. You were never there for me. While you didn't beat me, you were so verbally abusive to me that it made me feel like shit all the time."

"I kept you in line." This time she snorted. "Where is she? I want to know why she's changed the locks on our house. I need to get in and get some things out of it."

"Not without the police and Aunt Selma there you're not. Besides, it's not 'our' home. It's Aunt Selma's. She told me how you moved in with her like she needed you." Aunt Becky said she had. "Nope. Aunt Selma is a good deal stronger than you've ever given her credit for. Besides, I'm thinking you need to find yourself a home anyway. She's selling that one soon."

"Why would she—? You did that, didn't you? Just to see me on the streets. Well, I have money, so I can buy any home I want. You just wait and see." Rayne told her she didn't care if she had a house or not. "What a rude person you've turned out to be. My goodness, I should probably have beaten you once or twice to get that nastiness out of you. You should be nicer to me. I'm the only relative you have besides Selma. Did she tell you that she's dying? Well, she is."

"We're all dying, Aunt Becky. And you both being in your seventies isn't a big stretch in knowing that you're going to die too. But if you mean the cancer, yes, she told me about it. She also told me she's in remission. I have a feeling you would have left that part out had I not heard." Nothing. Not a denial or anything. "By the way, Grandda is fine as well. He's been having fun with our children. He said it makes him feel decades younger to be a great grandda."

"He should have died long ago, the old buzzard. He's just hanging on because he wants one of us to die first." She thought that was as good a reason as any and told her aunt that. "Have you always been a terrible person, or am I just noticing it?"

"Always have been. Always will be." She saw the surgeon coming down the hall. Charlie was just joining them in a wheelchair when he stopped to talk to them all. "I have to go. I'm not asking you for permission to hang up, Aunt Becky, because I know you well enough to not allow it. But I'll talk to you some other time."

Simply closing the connection, she stood up when Doctor Moran Davis sat across from Charlie. Since he and everyone else was going on the notion that she was Booker's wife, he was going to speak to her first.

"He's come through well. The bullet didn't do much damage. But he will need to rest up and behave himself for the next week or so. He had a lot of injuries and is lucky his head is hard." He looked at Wats. "I did take a look at his head. You're right. It was a good sized gash. I opened it up while I was in the sterile room and washed it out while I had him under. I hope you don't mind that I did that."

"No. I'm glad you did it. I don't want anything to happen to him." Wats looked relieved. "I was concerned when he wasn't arguing with us about bringing him in. He's not one to go to the doctor all that well."

"Well, he's in good hands, I believe." Doctor Davis looked at Charlie. "I'm to understand that you're going to be a physician here as well. You need anything, Charlie, you just let me know. I'm new as the head of this department, and I'm trying to make my way into getting things on a better standing between doctors and nurses. If you need anything, I'm serious, you just call me or come by."

It was another hour before they got to see Booker. Rayne could tell he was in a great deal of pain, so when he was taken to his room, sharing it with Charlie, she rushed the rest of them out of the room so he could get some meds and rest. Yes, Rayne thought this was a good family to be in with.

Louis was holding Wesley's hand when he got off the elevator. It was a good sight to see, the two of them. When he saw her, he came to her slowly. As soon as he was close enough, she gave him a big hug, then pulled out her phone to show him what they'd gotten for him today.

"The bunk beds will be nice if you want to

have someone stay over. And look at this old flag. I thought if you wanted to, you could hang it on your wall." He looked at the pictures as she showed him, and she knew he had questions. "If you don't like it, Louis, we can sort that out later. I just thought bunk beds would be nice for your new room."

"Are you going to send me back?" She asked him where she'd send him. "To my dad. He will come and get me. I don't ever want to go back there again. I like having stuff I can wear that is clean and stuff."

"I like you being there with us too, Louis. But in answer to your question, no, he's not going to get you again. They found your momma. Did you hear that?" He nodded. Louis had told the police that she had been buried in the back yard near the apple tree. "And Brenda is in jail too. They'll never get by any of us to get to you again. I swear to you on my life."

He played with her badge while he stood there next to her. She didn't rush him. The teachers she'd spoken to about Louis said he was a thinker and that if someone rushed him, he'd tighten up tighter than a rubber band around a wrist. When he did look up at her, she smiled at him when he grinned.

"Grandpa Wesley said him and me would go

fishing. I've never been, but when he told me he'd not been in years, I thought for sure he was kidding me." Rayne couldn't imagine the man with a fishing pole in his hand. "He told me if I wanted to, and I got good grades, him and me could have a lot of first times together. He even wants to go camping with me. I've slept outside before. I don't think it'll be the same with him, do you?"

"No. I'm sure you're going to have all the things necessary to make it a safe and fun trip. You might even make your food over an open fire." He warmed to that idea, then looked at her pictures again. "Do you not want the bunk beds?"

"No. I want them. That way, when Grandpa Wesley comes to read to me, we can rest up in the same room. He's pretty tired when he leaves me at night." She'd known Wesley was reading to Louis, just not that it had been nightly. "I'll be a really good boy for you, Mrs. Wilkerson. I promise you."

"I know that, Louis. But not too good, all right? I mean, we have to be able to ground you to the house so we can spend more time with you once in a while." She tickled him until he yelled for mercy.

When Wats joined her in their talk, she went to check on Charlie. She woke her up, she thought. "I'm sorry."

"Don't be. I was watching Booker." Coming into the room when asked, she stood by the bed so she could see how Charlie was doing. "I think my mom wouldn't be the least bit surprised that I fell for a Wilkerson. I mean, sheesh, she surely did talk about them a great deal. I'm so happy I'm going to be a part of this family that I could bust."

"I know how you feel." They both watched Booker breathing. "I just learned that you're going to have to keep an eye on Booker. He's sometimes a little stubborn when he's hurt and won't go to get checked out. They all have stories about him doing that."

"I will." Charlie took her hand into hers. "Thank you." Rayne asked her for what. "Not treating me like I wasn't good enough for him. For welcoming me to the family with open arms. I can't believe it's only been a few days, but I feel like I've known you all forever. It's a wonderful feeling."

"It really is."

She sat there with Charlie for a little while longer. As her eyes finally closed, she checked on Booker and left them there. She was glad to have a family like this one. Rayne would be on her toes to keep them healthy and well, but she was looking forward to that as well.

Before You Go...

HELP AN AUTHOR

write a review

THANK YOU!

Share your voice and help guide other readers to these wonderful books. Even if it's only a line or two, your reviews help readers discover the author's books so they can continue creating stories that you'll love. Log in to your favorite retailer and leave a review. Thank you.

AWARD WINNING, BESTSELLING AUTHOR

Kathi Barton, a winner of the Pinnacle Book Achievement award as well as a best-selling author on Amazon and All Romance books, lives in Nashport, Ohio, with her husband, Paul. When not creating new worlds and romance, Kathi and her husband enjoy camping and going to auctions. She can also be seen at county fairs with her husband, who is an artist and potter.

Her muse, a cross between Jimmy Stewart and Hugh Jackman, brings her stories to life for her readers in a way that has them coming back time and again for more. Her favorite genre is paranormal romance, with a great deal of spice. You can visit Kathi on line and drop her an email if you'd like. She loves hearing from her fans. aaronskiss@gmail.com.

Follow Kathi on her blog: http://kathisbartonauthor.blogspot.com/

www.ingramcontent.com/pod-product-compliance
Lightning Source LLC
Chambersburg PA
CBHW030224180626
46810CB00008B/2964